Dear Reader,

When I was sevent[...] rogue. You know th[...] sweet talk but little commitment. Somewhere during my senior year in high school my rogue asked me to marry him. Unable to see the inevitable future, I said yes, and after months of hot-and-heavy, he said, "I need to go out into the world and find myself...without you." Devastated, I vowed never to date again. Then I fell for another rogue, then another and another, until I thought for sure I was incurable.

Which brings us to Rudy Bellafini—the rogue poster boy. Although he's totally fiction, he's totally real to me and with my slightly quirky Italian heritage, it's no wonder there's a curse involved.

I'm not attracted to rogues anymore, just like I'm not attracted to expensive clothes and chocolate truffles.

Yeah, right!

Best,

Mary Leo

P.S. Please come visit me on my Web site at www.maryleo.net. We'll talk some more.

Cate looked sinful, but also elegant in her backless halter-style wedding gown

Her sister Gina had picked out the semi-designer creation and Mrs. Crocetti had discounted the dress for good luck. All was good.

"Let's take a second and hit the highlights." Gina's words made Cate stop before she left the room. "You're doing this revenge wedding because—"

"Because I don't want anything bad to happen to any other guy I may be interested in."

"And?"

"And this is the only way to break the curse. He jilted me ten years ago."

"And?"

"And because my last fiancé nearly choked to death on a cannoli."

"Makes perfect sense to me, but are you happy?"

"No."

"Great. Everything's as it should be."

Aunt Flo burst into the room. "What's the holdup, dolls? We got over a hundred people down there waiting for the bride. So are you going to walk down those stairs or are you going to jilt him now?"

For Better or Cursed

Mary Leo

HARLEQUIN®

TORONTO • NEW YORK • LONDON
AMSTERDAM • PARIS • SYDNEY • HAMBURG
STOCKHOLM • ATHENS • TOKYO • MILAN • MADRID
PRAGUE • WARSAW • BUDAPEST • AUCKLAND

ISBN 0-373-44192-4

FOR BETTER OR CURSED

Copyright © 2004 by Mary Leo.

This edition published by arrangement with Harlequin Books S.A.

® and TM are trademarks of the publisher. Trademarks indicated with ® are registered in the United States Patent and Trademark Office, the Canadian Trade Marks Office and in other countries.

www.eHarlequin.com

Printed in U.S.A.

ABOUT THE AUTHOR

For Better or Cursed is Mary Leo's follow-up novel to *Stick Shift*. She's had careers as a salesgirl in Chicago, a cocktail waitress and keno runner in Las Vegas, a bartender in Silicon Valley and a production assistant in Hollywood. She has recently given up her career as an IC layout engineer to pursue her constant passion: writing romance.

Mary now lives in Pennsylvania with her husband and new puppy.

To: Janet Wellington, for her endless energy;
Maureen Child, because she keeps me sane;
Cheryl Howe and Crystal Green, for their continued
encouragement; Holly Jacobs, who answers all
my lame questions; Rick, because he's rational
when I'm not; and most of all to Kathryn Lye,
the best editor a girl could have.

Prologue

There's a belief on Taylor Street in Chicago's Little Italy that if a man jilts a woman after a proposal of marriage, then her love life is forever cursed...unless, of course, the man returns so the woman can have her revenge.

RUDY BELLAFINI COULDN'T MOVE, at least not without agonizing pain, but as he lay in the snow, his skis pointing straight up in the air, a person stood over him snapping his picture.

"What the...?" Rudy said as he spit snow and debris out of his mouth, angry over the amateur paparazzo with the disposable camera.

"Don't worry about a thing, Mr. Bellafini." Click... "The ambulance is on its way." Click...click...click.

Rudy couldn't believe this chick. Did she have no shame?

"Come on. I'm a mess here. Could you stop with the pictures?" Rudy pleaded, and held up a hand to block the camera's focus.

Click... "Sorry, honey, but I thought guys like you loved this kind of stuff. Besides, it's an even trade. I called the ambulance. You owe me," she purred.

"I owe you? I'm lying here next to death and I owe you for calling an ambulance?"

"It's about giving something back."

"That would mean that I took something from you, which I didn't because I don't know you. Do I?"

Click...

"Stop taking—" Rudy mumbled, but the chick wouldn't give it up.

As Rudy dropped back in the snow, completely defeated, a curious memory drifted into his consciousness. A memory he thought he had successfully tucked away forever.

"Stop taking my picture," Rudy chided.

"I want to remember this when you're rich and famous," Cate said as she snapped several pictures of Rudy's face. They leaned up against the far wall in the back of his father's closed restaurant, teasing each other with kisses and laughter as a snowstorm howled right outside their door.

"You make me crazy," he said right before he kissed her gently on her full, wet lips.

"We came here for food," she taunted. "You told me that your dad left us a couple sandwiches."

"You are my food," he whispered between playful kisses.

She snapped another picture.

"I'm the one who's hungry. Not you. You ate like a pig today," she told him.

"I'm hungry for you," he said, not believing the words that came tripping out of his own mouth. All he knew at that exact moment was that he wanted her, right then, right there, and nothing could stop him. Her hair smelled like the rain, her skin tasted as sweet as sugar and her full breasts were softer than he had ever imagined. He had unbuttoned her sweater, and slipped her camisole off one shoulder to reveal her breast and now he couldn't keep his hands or his mouth away from her body.

"I thought you were in so much pain you couldn't move," she told him.

"I was, until you gave me that back and shoulder massage. I thought I wouldn't be able to ski again for the rest of the season. Then you came along. Did anybody ever tell you that you have the magic touch?"

"You're the first," she said, smiling.

"We should get married," he said after a deep kiss that sent a thrill through his entire body. He could feel her heat as she pressed up against him, leg twisted around his, arms surrounding his neck, his shirt undone so he could feel her breasts tickling his chest.

She pushed him back. "Are you asking me to marry you?"

He looked into her glistening brown eyes, saw that loving look on her sweet young face and answered a resounding, "Sure. Marry me, Cate Falco. Be mine forever. I'll give you all the gold and diamonds in the world."

"I don't want all the gold and diamonds in the world. A single strand of white gold and diamonds would do just fine. But we've only been dating for three months."

"Since when did dating-time have anything to do with marriage?"

"I don't know. Isn't it a rule or something? Aren't we supposed to get to really know each other first? I mean, we haven't even spent a whole night together, or had one decent argument. Aren't those the two main ingredients of happy marriages?"

"So that's it...sex and arguments? That's what makes a happy marriage?"

"I think so, and maybe a few thousand other things, but you obviously don't have time for the list. At least we should know..."

He kissed her again, then pulled back to continue on his quest.

"What's to know? You're the girl with the magical touch, and I'm the guy who needs a little magic in his life. Sounds like the perfect match to me."

"You're the one who's crazy. You know that?"

"You could be right, but let's get married, anyway."

She stared into his eyes as if she were searching for the right answer, then pulled him in tight and rested her head on his shoulder.

He hugged her even tighter, hoping for the right answer.

"So," she whispered.

He waited while she tickled his ear with her tongue, sending shivers right through him. He pulled his head away and looked at her, hoping, praying even, for a yes.

"So?"

Cate beamed with a smile that lit up her whole face. "So, yes. Of course I'll marry you. How could I not?"

He picked her up and twirled her around shouting, "Yes. Yes. Yes," as she snapped another picture of his smiling face.

"Yes, Cate, yes," he said out loud.

Two burly men from a rescue team picked Rudy up from the snow. "That's some dream you're having, Mr. Bellafini. But you need to relax now. You're going to be fine."

"Sure," Rudy said. "Relax. Like it's easy with your foot pointing in the wrong direction. Look at that. You should be on this stretcher, dude, trying to relax."

A woman from the same team, with black satin hair and pure brown eyes, a Latin angel, told him to breathe normally through the tubes poking into his nostrils. Rudy smiled and shut up long enough to finally lose all consciousness.

1

"IT's NOT YOU. It's me," Cate Falco said while sitting across from Joey Delano in the trendy dinner house on Michigan Avenue in Chicago. She watched as he tried to cut his rare steak with a blue cast wrapped around two of his fingers and halfway up his right arm.

"Come on. That's such a line," he said trying to get a grip on the knife.

"I know, but it's true. It really is me."

He put his flatware down and looked at her. "You're breaking up with me?"

"Yes," she answered in a cool, calm voice.

"But why? I thought we had a good thing going."

She thought this would go easier, but he looked seriously confused. "I'm thinking that since you met me, you've broken two fingers, fallen down a flight of stairs, got stuck in an elevator for five hours, sprained your wrist and got hit in the balls with some kid's baseball. I can't date you anymore. I'm a hazard to your health."

Cate sat back in her chair, getting a little weepy-eyed. She really liked this guy. He was funny, cute and got her weird sense of humor, but she just couldn't let it go on any longer.

"But they were all accidents. You weren't even there."

"I know, but believe me, this is for your own good."

"I don't get it."

"You know how everybody in Chicago believes the Cubs are cursed? Well, it can happen to people, too. I'm love-cursed and you're just experiencing the results."

"You expect me to believe this?"

Cate looked into his sweet brown eyes and said, "Yes."

"This is bullshit," he said.

It was at that exact moment that the waitress tripped while walking by, nearly dropping her tray of drinks in his lap.

"No, this is real. You're the last in a long line," Cate said. "I'm giving it up."

"What? You're not going to date anymore?"

"That's absolutely right. I'm embracing celibacy. I hear it's quite calming."

He stared at her for a long moment, then stood up, pulled some cash out of his pocket, slipped it under his plate and left.

Cate let out a heavy sigh.

THE NEXT MORNING Cate and her father, Ted, sat in their kitchen eating breakfast and reading the *Chicago Sun Times*. Ted ate soft-boiled eggs out of the shells, really-bad-for-you bacon, and vitaminless white toast, while Cate crunched on her completely-good-for-you bowl of organic Optimum power breakfast cereal with flaxseed, soy fiber, dried blueberries and 500 mg of OMEGA-3's.

They at least agreed on the coffee—Starbucks house blend, strong and black.

"Will ya get a load of this?" Ted announced with a flourish, tossing part of the paper across the table.

"What?" Cate asked as she picked up the sports section.

"Look whose mug is on the front page," he said while tightening the belt on his plaid robe. It was chilly in the large kitchen and her father not only wore a wool robe over flannel pajamas, but he liked to wear a white stocking cap on his balding head...to keep the heat in.

Cate took the paper, and there, spread across three columns was Rudy Bellafini, lying prone in the snow, looking absolutely awful. Aside from the fact that his body was the shape of a pretzel, his hair was way too long—shaggy and over his eyes, with a little curly flip just under his right ear—Cate wondered if the slight mustache and almost beard was due to a lack of shaving or if he had done it on purpose, for that scruffy-Hollywood effect.

She caught herself lingering over the picture a little too long. Cate purposely didn't react. A reaction would send her father into some lecture on "the guy who jilted you," and Cate didn't want to get into it, especially after last night.

"He never did like to get his hair cut," she said as she tossed the paper back to her father.

"That's all you got to say?"

"No. I'm sorry he's hurt." She took a big bite of her cereal. The crunching muffled her father's voice, but unfortunately, she could still make out what he was saying.

"He ain't just hurt. It says there that some girl named

Allison might'a pushed him off one of them ski chairs.''

"What does that have to do with me?"

"Because of him, you're thirty years old with no husband."

"I'm twenty-nine and I don't want a husband. I've got a good life just the way it is."

"You ain't got such a good life. He's got a good life. Winnin' all them gold medals, and for what? Slidin' down some bumpy hill. Who with a sane mind is gonna do that? Nobody, that's who."

"Those bumpy hills are called moguls, and it's an Olympic sport. You know that. You were glued to the TV every day during the games."

"Yeah, well it don't look like no sport to me. Skiing down a mountain like Alberto Tomba does is a sport. He's a champion. But them bumpy hills, that's no sport. It's just dumb."

She pushed herself up from the table. "No. This argument is dumb. I have to get to work. I'm booked all day."

But once her father started, there was no stopping him. "And what about them restaurants of his? He's made a million bucks on them bad Italian restaurants. What have you got? Sore hands."

"I like what I do. I'm a great therapist. I make a good living."

Cate leaned on the table ready to go at it with her father.

"Well, it ain't right for a single woman to be rubbing on some guy's hairy back all day. Only perverts and them weird sex people who like ropes and chains do that kind of stuff."

"Here we go!" She sat back down in her chair. "We've locked up all our ropes and chains. They leave marks."

"It wasn't so bad when you was going to school and working out in California. I don't know those people, but now that you got your own business right here in the neighborhood, I don't like it. I gotta see these people every day."

"Then don't go out."

"See what I mean? You don't care about the shame I gotta live under. It ain't right. You should be married to Rudy Bellafini and have a million bucks."

Cate grabbed her bowl and cup and put them in the sink. She hadn't really let herself think about Rudy in years, and now he was back, like lint in her dryer. "I have to go to work," she said, and kissed her father on the cheek.

"And tell that sister of yours it's time to get up. She does this every morning. Always late, that one."

Cate obeyed her father and knocked on Gina's door, but that was all she would do. She wanted to get out of there quickly and had no time to coax her sleepy sister awake. Not this morning. Not with Rudy Bellafini on the front page of the sports section.

As soon as Cate stepped out of the house, she walked straight to the newsstand on the next corner, bought her own copy of the paper and sat down on a cold, worn-out bench at the bus stop to read all about Rudy Bellafini, the man she never could shake. The man who had single-handedly cursed her entire adult love life. The putz.

The story read like it should have been inside a tabloid rather than a reputable newspaper. The focus of the piece was Allison Devine, Rudy's latest squeeze. According to insider sources, Allison had a temper that most of Hollywood tried to avoid. They listed her many outbursts: she had thrown a chair across a movie set; trashed several dressing rooms; assaulted an unnamed costar; and backed her BMW right into her last boyfriend's Ferrari. The article went on to say it was highly unlikely that Rudy had fallen without some assistance from the "Shrew of Hollywood."

As if anybody cares!

Cate threw the paper into the overflowing trashcan next to her and proceeded to walk to work. Part of her thought he deserved Allison Devine. She was perfect for him. Maybe they'd get married and live miserably ever after.

She could only hope.

But the other part of her wished he'd come back to Chicago, just once, so she could somehow expunge this curse thing and be done with Rudy Bellafini once and for all.

2

FORTUNATELY FOR RUDY nothing was actually broken, but the two-hundred-pound amazon therapist who currently pulled on his very sore legs only made matters worse. He had been in therapy for almost a week. Granted, he was older now, thirty-one, and it took longer for him to heal. His knees were shot, so he didn't expect much healing to go on there, but she really didn't know what she was doing.

"Dude, this is crazy. Do we really have to do this now?" Rudy asked in between bouts of shooting pain. He was on the floor lying across a very thin mat.

"It's good for the spine," she said, smiling at his agony.

"I've got a great spine. A perfect spine. It's my hip that's hurting."

"That's why I'm pulling on your leg."

"But it's my other hip."

"Oh," she said, and dropped his leg, then picked up the other one. The heel of his foot hit the mat with such force that it took all that was in him not to howl in pain.

"Look," he said trying to yank his leg away. "Could we do this some other time, like when you're at home and somebody else with more experience is on duty? I'm too tired for all this pulling and hurting right now."

"Nope. We have to do it now. Can't let that hip lock

up. I've got a whole routine planned for you. Once I finish with your leg, I move up to your neck."

"Look," he glanced at her name tag, "Linda. You seem like a nice enough girl, a little rough around the edges maybe, and it could be, a lot unprepared, but, hey, there's a whole group of guys who like rough, incompetent girls. Gives them a mission in life. Unfortunately, I'm not one of them. Let's get this straight. There's nothing wrong with my neck. It's my shoulder."

She stopped pulling and looked at the clipboard she had carried in. "That's not what it says on my chart."

"Well, your chart's wrong."

She flushed, then looked from left to right. "I'm sorry, Mr. Bellafini, but I'm not really a therapist. I work in the front lobby, but when I heard you were recovering here, I thought I could get the real story on how you fell off that lift. I mean, like, I don't want to be a receptionist forever. I'm studying to be a journalist. I go to night school. You're this week's assignment. So, tell me, Mr. Bellafini, did your girlfriend really push you off that lift?"

"No. It was an accident." But he wasn't so sure about that himself. Rudy tried to remain calm, tried to move away from her and ring for a nurse, but the red emergency alarm was in the middle of the wall, well out of his reach. "All I want is some rest. Can't a guy get some rest?"

"Sure, if you'll just answer a few of my questions. I'm your biggest fan. I was rooting for you when you won your first gold medal. By the way, when you hang all three medals around your neck, are they heavy?"

"Where's the nurse? Who let you in here?"

"Mr. Bellafini, please don't get upset. Just one little question." The woman straightened up, cleared her throat and said, "Is it true that you were caught messing around with some other Hollywood actress and that's why your girlfriend, Allison Devine, pushed you off the lift?"

She smiled at him and waited for her answer, as if he would actually give her one. Rudy stared at her, trying to imagine what kind of insanity ran through this woman's mind. When she opened her mouth to begin her next question, Rudy lost it. "Nurse," he yelled. "Help! Nurse!"

The journalist-in-training got scared and stood up, turned on her heels and quickly walked out of the rehabilitation room, carrying the chart but leaving Rudy sprawled across the mat, entirely unable to move.

IT HAD BEEN a little over a week since Cate had seen Rudy's picture in the paper, and so far she'd been unable to think of anything else. She blamed it on her new vow of celibacy. She was positive once she fell into the rhythm of this self-imposed, sex-depravation thing, all men would completely vanish from her thoughts, and she'd become as saintly as her aunt Flo, her mother's fifty-eight-year-old, silver-haired sister.

"I heard Joey's left nut blew up to the size of a melon," Aunt Flo said while she lay on her stomach on a table at Cate's Wellness Center.

Cate stopped the massage. "I'm not going to treat you if you keep this up."

Cate had been working on Aunt Flo's neck and shoulder every other day for the past month, but she still wasn't getting any better. Cate didn't know if the kink was real, or if Aunt Flo just wanted the attention. Cate was hoping for a little of both. She didn't want to believe that all her hard work wasn't helping.

"What?"

"Can we talk about something other than my love life?"

"Sure, doll. Anything you want."

Cate continued with the massage. "How about the weather? That's a neutral subject."

"What's to talk about? It's winter. There's not much conversation about ice and snow. And speaking of ice, at least you still got Henry O'Toole. He took care of Rocky pretty good. And come to think of it, you probably never would have met him if poor Rocky hadn't croaked on your wedding day."

"Rocky passed on, Aunt Flo. He didn't croak."

Cate speeded up her treatment. She wanted to get Aunt Flo out of there.

"You're right, but them undertakers sure do make good money, and he's Irish. The curse won't take him. And even if Henry is old enough to be your father, sometimes that's what a girl needs...another father."

"Henry's just a friend."

"They were all your friends, but you didn't love any of 'em but Rudy, that's your problem."

"My only problem is everybody telling me about Rudy Bellafini. He's gone and out of my life, and that's the way it is. Forever."

"So, we won't talk about him. Who is he, anyway? Just some boy who hurt my beautiful niece, that's all. Just the boy who stood her up at the altar, like that devil Pinky did to me thirty years ago. And now you and me both gotta carry the curse."

Cate refused to admit to anyone in her family that she actually believed in the curse. It just gave them more fuel.

"Rudy and I never made it to the altar. We set a date, that's all. He never even gave me a ring."

"I guess you're right." She paused for a moment, sighed and went on. "I mean, it don't matter that your first fiancé was in a hospital for three weeks when he got run over by the flower truck on your wedding day. Or that your second fiancé, may he rest in peace, Rocky Dilantano, the prizefighter, collapsed right there in church while you was walking up the aisle on your dear father's arm. It's a good thing your sweet mother isn't here to see all this, may she rest in peace, or she'd be worried sick, like me."

"Rocky had a bad heart, and stop worrying. I'm a big girl. I can take care of myself."

"You're right. Nothing to do with our curse. But, still and all, it's good to see that Rudy is getting what he deserves for jilting you."

Cate stopped and looked at her aunt. "I didn't get jilted."

"What do you call it, then?"

"Over," Cate said while gently tugging on Aunt Flo's arm.

"Excuse me," Gina Falco said as she leaned against the doorjamb of the private therapy room. Gina helped out at Cate's Wellness Center three days a week while she worked on her degree in sports medicine. Gina took after their mom, tall, slim, dark blue eyes and silky red hair that touched her tiny waist. The only thing she and Cate had in common was their height, everything else was completely different. Cate's eyes were amber, her hair short and brown with some blond highlights. She worked out a lot, so her figure was good, but she hated her big fat butt, and her too-small breasts, 34-B. And to top it all off, she had pulled out her first gray hair that very morning. Cate felt certain that soon she and Aunt Flo would look more like sisters rather than aunt and niece.

Cate turned to face Gina as she walked over and whispered in Cate's ear, "Rudy Bellafini just limped into the front office."

Cate pulled on Aunt Flo's arm with such force that the poor woman let out a glass-shattering yell, "Ee-yow!"

"Aunt Flo, I'm sorry," Cate said. "Are you all right?"

"What's the matter with you? Are you trying to kill me?" She scooted herself up and fluffed out her hairdo.

Gina said, "It's…it's our new method for getting rid of those really stubborn kinks. We learned it at the APTA conference last summer. No pain, no gain."

Cate rolled her eyes at her sister, knowing that Aunt Flo loved anything that sounded even remotely hip.

Aunt Flo rotated her shoulders, getting into a slow rhythm. Then she lifted her arms and said, "Well, why the heck didn't you try it sooner, doll. You know I play bunco at the church hall this afternoon with the ladies of Saint Mary's. They're probably waiting for me right now."

"He totally wants to see you, Cate," Gina interrupted.

"Tell him I'm with a patient. Tell him to come back tomorrow or next month or next year," Cate told her sister.

"You're not with a patient anymore. I feel grrreat! Just like Tony the Tiger. Who is it that wants to see you so bad and you don't want to see?"

"I thought you had a bunco game to get to." There was no way Cate would tell Aunt Flo that Rudy Bellafini was in the building. It would be all over the neighborhood in the time it took for Cate to exhale, which she had forgotten to do.

Gina broke in, "I put him in room three, Cate. The guy can barely walk. Maybe you should at least talk to him."

"It's bad luck to turn a potential patient away, especially somebody who can't walk. Anything could happen. Your sister herself could be struck down."

"All right, already! I'll talk to him," Cate said, trying desperately to hold on to her composure. She turned to her aunt. "The ladies of Saint Mary's are waiting."

"Heck, they sure are. Oh, well, I'll get the skinny from your father tonight at dinner. Now go. You don't want to keep the poor man waiting," she said as she shooed Cate away.

As Cate walked down the narrow hallway to room three, her stomach felt a little queasy and her knees didn't want to bend the way they were supposed to. Her palms were sticky, and suddenly her whole body broke out in a cold sweat.

When she reached the dreaded door number three, she paused in front of it to regain her composure and fix her hair. And what about her makeup? It had to be a mess by now. And the sweater she threw on earlier, it had holes in the right sleeve.

She rushed back to her office, thinking that she needed a complete makeover before she could see him.

That she required a new do from Rose Marie at The Hairs End, or a new outfit from Gloria's Dress Boutique, or maybe a couple sessions with Frank Nudo, the shrink at the end of the block, before she could say one word to Rudy Bellafini. Or Father Joe, he would know how to handle the situation. Or Henry...no, not Henry, he was only good with dead people.

She wished she could talk to Gina, but Gina was busy at the front desk...that in itself was possibly a good thing. She didn't need Gina knowing that she was in a pathetic panic to suddenly re-create herself.

As if...

She picked up the phone, ready to call her father—of all people—just as Rudy Bellafini appeared in her open doorway. He looked completely helpless and miserable while leaning on his crutches. He crumpled himself into the black chair next to the door and sat down, letting out a long, pathetic moan.

3

"YOU LOOK BEAUTIFUL, Cate. Time's been on your side, dude." He gave her the once-over, like he was sizing her up for some TV reality show and he was the latest bachelor. "I don't see a ring on your finger. I thought for sure you'd be married with five kids."

Cate raised an eyebrow. "And I thought for sure you'd be on your fifth wife."

"Not likely."

They stared at each other for a moment. This was not a good beginning, Cate thought.

Rudy continued, "Okay. We should get started right away. You'll need to cancel all your appointments for the next few weeks. Maybe longer. I need you to concentrate on me. I'm in pretty bad shape, here, and I can't afford to be down for too much longer. I'll pay whatever you want, just so I know that I'll have your undivided attention. Whatever you need in the way of equipment, you got it. Just let me know what it is. This whole thing has to be kept a secret or, believe me, your life will turn into a nightmare, as well as mine. Here are my medical records, dude." With some effort he tossed the large manila envelope on her desk.

She was a *dude* now? Cate didn't know how to respond to *dude*.

He continued, "I think that about covers it. Dude, I'm really hurting, but that room I was in is way too small." He took a breath and pushed himself up from his chair with an obvious grimace of pain on his face. "You have anything bigger?"

Cate was actually dumbstruck by the burst of orders that he'd flung in her direction. She couldn't react properly to the magnitude of his arrogance. She didn't quite know how to respond to her new charter, so she sat back in her chair and watched as he hobbled out of the office apparently expecting her to follow, but she didn't.

She waited for the shock of him to wear off. Perhaps then she would actually be able to think.

"Hel-lo. Anybody in there? Which door do I go through?"

Her brain finally came around as he reappeared in the doorway. "The front door, *dude*. And don't let it hit you on the way out," she said, flashing a sarcastic grin.

For a brief moment she had considered shuffling him off to one of the other therapists who worked for her, but she couldn't justify dumping his snotty self on anybody.

"Don't kid around, Cate. I'm in a lot of pain here. The sooner we get started the sooner I can get my life back."

"You can get back to your life right now," she said. "Don't let me get in your way."

"What's wrong with you? Didn't you hear my offer?"

"I heard it, but I'm not for sale."

"I'm not buying you. I'm buying your services."

"I am my services, and as long as these two hands are attached to my two arms, I'm not for sale."

Rudy hobbled back into the office and sat down

again, gently. His breathing had increased, and he looked unsettled, but his arrogance had defined the moment. If she could physically kick him out of her office and onto the street and watch him hit the pavement with a thud, she would at least feel as though they were once and for all even.

But she couldn't.

He was taller than she had remembered, and maturity had thickened his body. Not that he was fat, he had merely turned into a man, with deep-brown eyes, darker than she remembered, and thick black hair, blacker than she remembered. It's not that she hadn't seen him on TV and on magazine covers, or cereal boxes over the years, but to see him up close again was just different. He actually looked even more handsome in person, and that bad-boy arrogance she thought was just for the media was actually real.

Too bad.

"Look, I know I'm vulnerable right now, and you can hold out for any amount of money you want, but I have my limits."

"I don't want your money."

He chuckled. "Of course you do. Everybody does, but I've gotten used to the greed factor."

"I think you need to leave now."

"Come on, Cate. It's me, Rudy." His determination didn't waver. "What? You're still mad about what happened seven years ago?"

"Ten. It was ten years ago. And do you honestly think I gave you a second thought?"

"Good, then why won't you treat me? Isn't there some kind of law about therapists and patients? Some kind of code you people live by? How can you turn me away?"

"I don't know. How can I? I must have rocks for brains. Or maybe I just don't like you and your full-of-yourself self."

"Excuse me?"

"There is no excuse. Please leave, which is something you're good at."

He didn't say anything. He just stared at her with a look of confusion on his face.

She stood up.

He stood, albeit slowly.

"I'm sorry you feel this way, Cate. I could have used your magic touch."

His words brought back the memory of the night he proposed, which only made her more angry.

"What a crock! That line's stale. Don't you have a new one?"

"I never should have come back here. I knew you'd be like this. You never could just accept things."

"Accept things! So, I should have just accepted the fact that you walked out on me?" She crossed her arms over her chest.

"Like I had a choice? It was my once-in-a-lifetime chance. You wouldn't have come with me."

Her anger welled up with his words. "You never asked."

"Asked you to do what? Give up your scholarship to UCLA and come follow me around to some training camp? Yeah, that would've worked out. Not likely." His face softened and he took a step toward her. "Cate, I—"

"Just go," she said, her voice shaking. "This debate

is far too stressful, and I've been working on calm. I'm sure you can get all the therapy you need back in Rudyworld."

"Yeah. Well, if you change your mind, I'll be over at my parents' old brownstone. I'm going to hang around for a while. Get it fixed up. Feel free to drop by any-time."

He hobbled out of her office while she stood waiting to hear the front door on the Wellness Center close so she could sit down and scream.

THE BROWNSTONE where Rudy had spent his teenage years with his mom and dad had all but been deserted. His parents, Betty and Sam, now lived in Florida, com-plements of Rudy, and journeyed back to Chicago only when they had to, which in the past five years had been only once, when old man Barcio died. Tony Barcio had been their landlord and good friend. Rudy had bought the place as soon as it came on the market. He really didn't know why he bought it, but at the time it had seemed like the right thing to do for his mom and dad, or maybe just for himself.

Now as he sat alone in the empty house, he won-dered what the hell he was doing. Why had he per-sisted in returning to his old neighborhood?

There were some pictures hanging on the walls. Pic-tures of his mom and dad in Florida, a couple aunts and uncles, a picture of himself wearing his gold med-als, but there was one picture that really threw him a curve ball. It was a picture of his cousin, Pete.

Rudy had always admired Pete because he actually knew what he wanted to be from the time he was a lit-tle boy, a wooden-furniture craftsman. Rudy only knew one thing—escape—and he would do whatever it took to achieve it. Marrying Cate had meant putting down roots and building a life together. When that reality had finally taken hold, he'd freaked and run to the nearest exit.

His excellent freestyle skiing ability bought him a ticket with one of the best moguls coaches in the country. After he achieved what he wanted there, he went into the restaurant business. Lately his restaurants were starting to bore him. He could never stay in one place, or with one thing, for too long. Even his house in Malibu had lost its appeal, but he didn't know where to escape to this time, or to what, exactly.

Pete had stayed right where he grew up, a small town in Wisconsin, had four kids, his own business and according to the picture on the wall, a pretty little wife.

Rudy had his own business, three gold Olympic medals, enough money to last him his entire lifetime and a silver-framed picture of Allison Devine, Hollywood's latest ingenue, on his desk. The woman who had, in fact, pushed him right out of that lift.

Pete was happy.

Rudy was happy...yeah, right.

Now, as he sat in his dad's green recliner in the living room waiting for the house to get to a more livable temperature, he pondered whether it had been a smart move to let his driver leave. After the cold shoulder he had received from Cate, which he certainly deserved, he hadn't been able to think straight. And to make matters worse, he was freezing and hungry, and his cell phone had gone completely dead, but he hurt too much to get up to try to find the charger.

The brownstone was a dusty, spider-infested, cold, dark mess and unless there was some major work on it ASAP it was totally uninhabitable. All the furniture, what there was of it, was covered in sheets that had long ago lost their protective power. Cobwebs hung in every corner. What wasn't covered had a thick blanket of dust and grime. The walls were a lovely shade of soot.

At least the heat worked and the place had electricity, two things that Rudy had kept on.

The doorbell rang.

"Come in," he yelled. "It's open."

"Hellooo," a high-pitched, female voice echoed throughout the house as the front door creaked open. "Betty? Sam? Is that you?" the voice asked.

He couldn't see who it was because the front door was on the other side of the wall in the hallway, but the voice was familiar.

"I'm in here," he yelled, anxious to see his visitor, hoping against all hope it was Cate.

Okay, so yeah, he had been somewhat rude, but those eyes of hers, those big, dark, wonderful eyes were even more fantastic than he had remembered. He had searched for some compassion in them, but there wasn't any, so he simply lashed out. Probably not his best move, given the circumstances.

And the way her bottom lip curled when she got angry. Perfect.

He sat up straight, ready to apologize, ready to bear his soul, to discuss the past in a more reasonable tone, when some other woman turned the corner into his living room.

"What a dump!"

At first Rudy didn't recognize the round, middle-aged woman in the bright-red coat and matching red scarf. Then, as his memory spun back several years, ten to be exact, he knew precisely who was standing in front of him.

"Hello Aunt Flo," he quipped. Everyone in the neighborhood knew Florence Adriana Lucille Del-Veccio as Aunt Flo, and Rudy was no exception.

"Little Rudy Bellafini, as I live and breathe. You, of all people. I never thought I'd see your face in this part of town again. What on earth are you doing here?" she asked while holding on to her Marilyn Monroe beaded handbag. Aunt Flo's nose and cheeks matched the color of her outfit, bright red, causing Rudy to grin despite her somewhat rude remark.

"Hey, Aunt Flo, it's good to see you." He shifted his weight to his other hip, wincing as a shooting pain went from his shoulder to his right big toe. He could actually feel pain in his big toe. He wanted to rip off his shoe and rub it, but thought better of it as he stared at Aunt Flo's contorted face, obviously already disgusted by the condition of the house. "I'd get up, but as you can see, I'm somewhat indisposed at the moment."

"I don't know about the disposal part, but you're a mess. For all your money, and I heard you got a bundle, what are you doing sitting all alone in this rat trap? Are you here to make things right with my niece?"

"Well, I..."

"You don't gotta say any more. I can tell that you got other reasons." She put her gloved hand over her mouth and drew in a loud breath, "Did that Allison clean you out and now all you got left is this dump?" She gasped.

"Aunt Flo, relax. I've got plenty of money."

"Well, at least that's something, but for a man who says he's got plenty of money, you sure are peculiar. You look skinny. Pale. You should eat something, you'll feel better."

"Thanks, but..."

"Come on out with me. We can talk and you can buy me a nice hot meal with all this money you still got." She started toward him.

Rudy wanted to join her. He tried to get up from the dilapidated chair, but with each movement the recliner seemed to engulf him.

"Tell you what, I got my mobile phone. My Cate got it for me last Christmas. She's a wonderful girl, that Cate. You shoulda never done what you did, but we'll talk about that later." She smiled, but Rudy didn't exactly like the look on her face. "She's beautiful and generous and good-hearted, not like some of them loser women you run with. A good-looking boy like you shouldn't..."

She dug through the Monroe purse. "Where the heck is it? I only use the thing for emergencies, all that talk about brain tumors and stuff. Your dad thought Betty caught a brain tumor from the mobile phone. Even took her to the Mayo Clinic because she was acting so mean all the time. Turned out she was going through *the change*, but still, you can't be too careful these days." She pulled a checkbook, a notebook and an industrial-size wine opener out of her purse, peeked in and shouted, "There it is, way on the bottom."

She plucked out the shiny red phone and showed it to Rudy, cradling it in her hands as if she were presenting it for purchase. Aunt Flo had worked at Marshall Fields ever since she was sixteen years old, and probably still did. Back when Rudy knew her, she had always prided herself on her sales abilities. "An important man like you should get himself one of these. This is the Superturbo F720k. Great little phone, even takes pictures. I haven't quite figured out how to use that feature yet, but a smart man like you could probably figure it out without the directions."

She went on about some of the other features while Rudy thought about his aching big toe, the absurdity of the situation he found himself in, the pain in his hip, his leg and, most of all, his neck.

Then, sometime right before he was about to let out an earth-shattering moan, Aunt Flo sat down next to him on a rickety chair. "Don't you worry about a thing," she told him in a vanilla voice. "Let's see now," she said. "I know just the person to call to come get us out of this hell hole."

4

"MARRY ME. Tonight. Make all my dreams come true." Henry yelled from the dining room as he set the dark-walnut table for eight, something Cate did every night. She liked being prepared for inevitable company. "A woman who can cook, these days, is a rare find. Be mine and you can cook for me every night."

How could a woman refuse such an offer?

Cate plunked the wooden spoon she held into the tomato sauce and wiped her hands on her apron. "No, thanks, Henry," Cate yelled back from the kitchen. "I'm not ready to get married tonight. I have to wash my hair. But thanks for asking...again."

It had been the third proposal that week. They were coming faster now. The only reason Cate could think of for the sudden surge was that Henry was turning fifty soon. Maybe he was on a self-imposed deadline to remarry, and she fit the job description:

Wanted: desperate female who can cook and likes to be around dead people all day. Will marry for food.

Just as Cate walked into the dining room carrying a plate of ricotta-filled canolli, Henry's favorite dessert, and picturing the ad in the *Sun Times* personals, Gina burst into the house along with an amazingly strong gust of wind off the lake.

The wind toppled Henry's towering floral centerpiece. Lilies, pink carnations and roses blew across the table, and the lovely pea-green vase that Henry had brought over from his funeral home the previous week cracked with the fall. Cate turned on her heel and went back into the kitchen for a dish towel.

"Hi, Henry," Gina said. "Too many roses, Henry. Cate hates roses. Where is she? I think we broke her ex and we need her to get the pieces out of the car."

"What's the matter?" Cate asked, as she walked back out of the kitchen. She tossed the dish towel to Henry, who just stood there staring at the mess on the table. His face almost always had that startled look to it, as if he lived in a constant state of surprise. Perhaps it was the way his jet-black eyebrows arched above his cobalt-blue eyes, and the contrast of his thick, totally white hair, and the way his nostrils flared like he was desperate to take in air, or maybe it was that last face lift.

"Cate, it's not my fault," Gina insisted. "The guy doesn't listen to reason. He's more stubborn than Dad. I told him not to get into the back seat."

"What are you talking about?"

"He's stuck, Cate, and can't move. Our car ate his foot."

"Call cousin Charlie. He's pushing three-hundred pounds. He'll get your boyfriend out of the car."

"He's not my boyfriend, Cate. He's yours. And Charlie's already out there."

Henry looked over at Cate. "You have a boyfriend?"

"Why didn't you say so?" Cate grabbed her coat and hurried out the front door ahead of Gina. Henry followed but stopped in the doorway, holding on to part of his floral centerpiece. "Wait," he yelled. "Was it the roses? Women love roses. Don't they?"

As soon as Cate stepped out into the cold night air and took one look at the twisted man caught inside the classic, faded orange-colored VW Beetle, she knew he was in real trouble. Complete sympathy overtook her like a mud bath and swirled in thick waves of human compassion.

Cate and Gina shared the car, but it was actually Cate's, only she hardly drove it anymore. Most of the time she would grab a bus or a train to get where she was going. Gina had commandeered the Bug to get back and forth from school on a daily basis.

Cate only caught a glimpse of Rudy's tortured face as cousin Charlie pulled on Rudy's arms, apparently attempting to rip them right off his body. It was the high-pitched yelp that gave the painful maneuver away.

"Stop it," Cate yelled as she stood in front of the car parked next to the curb. They were all there, most of the neighborhood, and most of her family, each trying to unwedge the unwedgeable from both sides of the car.

In all the chaos, she noticed that Aunt Flo and her dad were actually holding hands...almost as if they were a couple. She immediately turned away and pushed her attention to Rudy. The thought of Aunt Flo and her dad as a couple was absolutely ridiculous, and she didn't even want to consider it.

When she looked again, they had stopped holding hands. Now they stood well apart from each other.

That was better. She thought perhaps it had been a lighting thing, or maybe she hadn't seen it at all? Convincing herself that it was just the confusion of the moment, she went on to more urgent issues.

"You guys have to stop," she told everyone. They instantly backed off.

When Cate stuck her head in the car, Rudy smiled up at her like a helpless puppy. He sat in the back seat, sideways, with one leg stretched out along the seat and the other one hidden somewhere in front of him. His arms draped over the front seat as if they were no longer part of his body.

"Hurt much?" she asked.

"Only while I'm awake," he said.

"So, tell me, only kids and small animals fit in this back seat. Which did you think you were?"

"I got hungry."

"Rosebuds delivers."

"Aunt Flo had other plans."

"Oh, so this is Aunt Flo's fault. Then why isn't she in the back seat?"

"I was being a gentleman."

"Don't say that too loud, I might hear you and get the wrong idea."

He smiled. "Look, Cate, I'll do anything you want, just don't let cousin Charlie near me."

She had to smile back. He looked too cute. "So tell me, Sir Gallant, aside from your general maladies, why can't you get out of here?"

"My foot is stuck under the front seat."

"Not quite as much room back there as your limo, huh?"

"Do you ever stop?"

Cate dropped her gaze for a moment and took a breath, and that's when she remembered the problem with the front passenger seat. It had a bolt missing and a gaping hole in the slider thing. If you put anything near it or around it when someone slid the seat back, that anything would get gobbled up. She'd lost a new pair of shoes once and it had torn a pair of Gina's best pants right off her leg just two weeks before.

Both Gina and Cate had intended to have their dad fix it in his body shop, but neither of them had made the effort to get it over to him, and as long as no one sat in the back seat...so much for that theory.

She looked up again, and was about to tell him the missing-bolt story, but he was staring at her. He had the most gorgeous eyes, with thick long eyelashes, and the way his hair fell across his forehead reminded her of the reason she had fallen in love with him in the first place. Rudy had the ability, with just one sweet look, to make a girl believe everything he said.

It was that other Rudy, the evil-twin Rudy, who had been in her office earlier; aggravating her temper, causing irrational behavior in an otherwise completely rational person. *He* was the Rudy she knew.

"You're right," she said. "I'm sorry. So...you're stuck."

"A temporary condition, I'm sure." He twisted himself around to face the front.

Aunt Flo stuck her head in the car. "Your dad says we're gonna have to call the fire department. Vinney McCally is on tonight. He knows how to work them Jaws of Life."

"That might be a little extreme and I've got..." Cate said, but before she could finish her sentence the sound of sirens echoed through the neighborhood.

"Oops, too late," Aunt Flo declared and pulled herself out of the car to look down the street. Cate stepped out, as well.

"Ya know, it's times like these that I don't blame Rudy for leaving this place," Cate told her aunt.

Rudy rolled down the back window. "Tell me there's an actual fire somewhere and that sound isn't for me," he said with genuine concern in his voice.

Cate smiled down at him, then turned away as the hook-and-ladder pulled up alongside the tiny car and three burly firemen jumped out, Vinney McCally being one of them.

"It's for you," she told Rudy.

Rudy sat back and sighed.

Vinney walked over to Cate, dressed in complete catastrophe gear. "Cate, is it the old man? Don't worry about a thing. I'm here now. Where is he, Cate? It's gonna be all right."

Vinney McCally was one of those short but powerful kind of guys. The gymnast type who worked out more than he should and had to buy his clothes three sizes too big just to fit across his double-wide chest.

Cate had dated him for a little while until he started talking marriage. That's when a tree fell on him one Sunday afternoon in Lincoln Park while he walked his mother's schnauzer.

The schnauzer got away without a scratch, but Vinney was pinned under a limb for two hours. When it was all over and he was lying on a table in the emergency room with a fractured pelvis and a broken arm, Vinney whispered into Cate's ear, "I'm breaking up with you. Please go home and take your curse with you."

It was during that time, while he lay there in a broken heap, that he decided to become a Chicago fireman. He told everyone that if he could survive dating

Cate Falco, he could certainly survive fires and dangerous accidents.

"It's not my father. It's Rudy Bellafini. He's trapped
in the back seat," she explained.

"Get out!" Vinney said as he hunkered down to get
a better look inside.

Rudy smiled and finger waved.

"What d'ya know. Now, that's a guy I never thought
I'd see in this part of town again. But what's he doin' in
the back seat of your car?" Vinney asked and waved
back at Rudy. "You got him trapped in there or somethin'? Trying to get your revenge?"

"No. He did it on his own. His foot is stuck."

"Geez, Cate. That curse thing just don't want to let
you go, huh? He didn't propose again, did he?"

Cate's temper reared up and she lashed out.

"No, Vinney. There were no proposals. He's just
stuck. Can't a guy get his foot stuck without it being re-
lated to some damn curse?"

"Hold on. Don't have a coronary. I was only kid-
din'."

He leaned inside the open door on the driver's side
of the car. "Hey, man. How ya doin'? It's been a
while." They shook hands.

"Been better," Rudy said. "Can you get me out of
here, dude?"

Cate had to smile watching laid-back Vinney deal
with uptight Rudy.

"Oh, sure, man. Don't worry about a thing. We'll
have you outta here in no time."

"Can we do it before the press finds out?"

"They ain't gonna find out if I don't tell 'em, now are
they?"

"Thanks, dude. I owe you one."

"Just doing my job, man. Now let's see what's going on under there." He turned around and yelled for one of the other firemen to get a light, and suddenly the whole street lit up like the sun had just come out.

FOR THE NEXT TWO HOURS, Vinney and his rescue team from the Loomis Street Station worked to set Rudy free.

In the end the front passenger seat had to be removed through the roof, which, of course, required a hole. Cate actually cried a little when she saw the roof come off and the seat come out in tiny pieces.

"Don't worry about it," Aunt Flo said, as chunks of Cate's car hit the pavement with a sharp clank. "Rudy told me he's still got plenty of loot. He'll get you a brand-new one of them bug cars."

The '79 classic Beetle had more sentimental value than retail value, so the replacement idea had little impact. Cate had bought it secondhand when she was a teenager. She had worked a whole year in a hot bakery and saved every dime. She loved that car and had a hard time lending it to her sister...who had promised to take good care of it, which, until Rudy Bellafini came along, she had.

But it wasn't her sister's fault, it was Cate's. She was sure of it now.

When Rudy finally came limping out of the car, using Vinney's right arm for support, the group, which now consisted of the entire neighborhood plus a couple of lost tourists, cheered.

A male paramedic checked out Rudy's foot. Cate could tell Rudy was anxious about something, which was good. The sooner she could get him into that ambulance, the better.

"Can you walk?" the paramedic asked.

"I think so. I just want to get inside somewhere."

He started to take a step but he stumbled. Vinney grabbed Rudy under one arm for support, and the paramedic grabbed the other.

"Easy there, fella. Put your weight on me," Vinney commanded, his tone official. That was something Cate wasn't used to. It gave her a new sense of respect for her former boyfriend.

"I guess I'm in worse shape than I thought," Rudy said with a slight edge to his voice.

"Maybe you should lie down. Take it easy. You might do better at the hospital," Vinney told him.

"I've had enough of hospitals. They can kill ya. No telling who they let in there. I'll call a cab and go back to my dad's old house. I'll be fine there," he said, but then gazed over at Cate with his "save me" look that she never could refuse.

"Bring him inside," she told Vinney, guilt oozing into her reasoning. She told herself it would just be for a few hours, just until he was steady on his feet.

"But—" Vinney started to say.

Cate broke in. "He'll be fine. Nothing's broken."

"Whatever you say." Vinney helped Rudy across the lawn and up the stairs. Gina led the way, opening doors and moving anything and anybody in their path.

"We'll put him down in a chair in the living room for now," Cate said, but the living room was crowded with neighbors admiring Henry's indoor garden, and the dining room was filled with hungry relatives, so they took him to the one place in all the world where

Cate thought she would never, ever see Rudy Bellafini again.

Vinney walked him up the stairs to Cate's bedroom and put him right down in the center of her queen-size, antique, walnut bed.

5

RUDY REMEMBERED all the times he had sneaked up to this bedroom when they were dating, and wondered if he was lying on the same mattress they had made love on countless times.

God she was hot.

It was essentially the same room. Frilly and girly, just the way he liked it.

Of all the bedrooms in all the world, I had to walk, okay, hobble back into this one.

"Hope that foot don't give you too much trouble," Vinney said. "Say, if you're gonna be around for a while, come on over on a Friday night. Got a card game going with some of the old gang. Love to get my hands on a little of that dough I been hearing about."

"I don't know. I'm not much of a gambler," Rudy said with a dismissive tone. "But, hey, thanks for everything, dude." He stuck out his hand for a closing handshake. Vinney took it and gave him one of those heartfelt shakes, making Rudy feel a bit uneasy. He pulled his hand away.

"Well, I better go," Vinney said.

"Don't start any rumors, Vinney McCally. He's only in here because there was nowhere else to put him," Cate snapped.

Vinney raised an eyebrow, smiled and lumbered out of the room, dragging his black-booted feet as he went.

"He's still the same slow guy," Rudy said once Vinney was out of earshot.

"He just pulled you out of a bad situation and that's all you can think of to say about him?"

"No. I was just saying—"

"Well, don't be. Vinney's a hero."

"I never said he wasn't," Rudy said, feeling totally awkward. If he could be anywhere at that moment, it would *not* be in Cate's bed. At least not like this...with her lying next to him, naked, perhaps...but not when he was completely immobile and as helpless as a kid. The mental visual of Cate's naked body gave him a total body rush, and when Cate leaned over to remove his shoes he felt excitement in his groin. He liked everything about the situation, until she dropped his foot, hard, on the bed.

The flush of excitement immediately vanished. What was it lately with angry women and his feet? "Look, I'm sorry about what I said or didn't say about Vinney."

He could see her anger soften. At least he had said the right words that time.

"Let me get you a couple aspirins. They should help with the pain. If it gets worse, I have something stronger. I'll be right back," she told him, and left the room.

Rudy had to admit that his body hurt like hell, but it already felt a little better to be in a prone position. He pulled another one of the pillows under his head and looked around. The girl still had a thing for pink.

He pushed himself up on his elbows so he could check himself in a mirror above the dresser.

"See anyone you like?" Cate asked.

He jumped with the sound of her voice.

"You shouldn't sneak up on a guy like that, especially in my condition."

She smiled, sat down next to him on the bed and handed him three aspirin and a glass of water. "Here. This should take care of your *condition*."

He dutifully took the pills.

"Try to relax. It's been a long day."

Rudy was unexpectedly overcome with emotions for Cate, for their past, for his walking out on her and for how much he would like to just kiss her. Right there on her bed, the way he used to. He could almost feel her lips on his. "Look, Cate, I want to tell you how sorry I am about your car. I'll have another one here tomorrow morning. Would a Lexus be all right?"

Cate smiled her apparent approval. "A Lexus would be fine."

"And, Cate, I want to thank you for taking me in like this." He was watching how she moved. How she looked, and that butt of hers. Outstanding. "And, I want to—"

He tried to get the words out, but he didn't know where to begin. They needed to talk. "I want to tell you—"

"That you're sorry for..."

That was it. He would tell her that he was sorry for everything. Women liked it when you gave them a blanket apology, but she interrupted him before he could say anything.

"...the way you treated me this afternoon."

"Yes."

God, she has the best mouth.

"Yes, what?" she asked.

"This is ridiculous. I have something important I want to tell you." Just then he had a powerful recollection of how her lips felt on his.

Warm.

How she tasted.

A little sweet.

How her body fit under his.

Perfectly.

"So, then, say it," she said. Her lips puckering with the word *so*.

She abruptly stood up, breaking his lip trance, put her hands on her hips and waited.

The moment had obviously passed.

"Do you want something to eat?" she asked.

"Sure."

"I'll get you some pasta. The tomato sauce is good for you. It's loaded with vitamin C and lycopene." She turned and walked away.

"No. Don't go, Cate."

She turned back around in the doorway. "You can tell me what you want to say after you eat. My mom used to say that apologies are always easier on a full stomach. I think she was right."

"I'm sorry about your mom, Cate."

"Thanks."

But she'd gone before he could holler wait.

He really did want to tell her how sorry he was that he had skipped out on her. Explain a few things. How he'd been uncertain about marriage. Back then he couldn't think past the moment, let alone a lifetime. She had her whole life planned out, all he had was a dream.

He had used skiing as an excuse for his escape—she

wouldn't understand his passion. She'd want babies and a mortgage. So he ran, but he never stopped loving her. Never stopped thinking about her. He knew for a fact that she was the reason why he'd been so good at the moguls game. Every time the competition got tough, he'd think of Cate and work harder at the sport to erase her from his thoughts. He'd been so certain she'd gotten married to some other guy, and now to find out she hadn't really sent him spinning.

He couldn't figure her out. Women like Allison, he was all over, but Cate was in a league of her own.

He'd like to tell her that his leaving had been for some noble cause, like he was saving her from his un-committable self or something equally as honorable, but he wasn't up to lying to Cate.

Not now.

Not when she had actually taken him into her home and he was lying in her bed. He suddenly wished he could go back in time and change his obviously wrong-headed decision.

CATE MADE HER WAY down the hallway past Gina's bedroom, then past her mother's old room, and started down the stairs.

The voices from the dining room echoed through the narrow stairway. Dinner for six or eight had appar-ently turned into dinner for the neighborhood.

Usually she liked a houseful of family and friends, but not tonight, especially now when her emotions were running around making her say and do stupid things. Who was that girl out on the front lawn who'd invited Rudy Bellafini into her house? Into her bedroom? And into her bed? It certainly wasn't the same Cate who threw him out of her office that afternoon.

Guilt. That's what drove her. Guilt over her car and her refusal to work on his battered body. He was right. She had been unprofessional about the whole thing.

But he was so full of himself.

The group sitting around the table was rather loud, everyone talking at the same time about totally different subjects. Her Dad sat in his usual spot at the head of the table, while everyone else squeezed in where they could.

Gina was there, along with Henry, Vinney and his rescue team, cousin Charlie, a few neighbors and the lady from Henry's funeral home who could never stop crying. Henry once dated her when they were in high school, but they broke up right after graduation. The details were always somewhat sketchy.

Cate slipped right past everyone and headed into the kitchen.

"I almost got it ready," Aunt Flo said, standing over two massive bowls of pasta. She ladled on the thick red sauce from the giant stainless steel pot sitting on the kitchen table.

"I added a few more tomatoes, a little bit more basil, some more garlic, a couple sprigs of parsley, and what do ya know, we got more than enough to feed this bunch."

"It looks good, but why is everybody here? Don't they have homes of their own?"

Aunt Flo spooned on the freshly grated Parmesan cheese. "Suddenly you got a problem with your friends and family around your dinner table?"

"No...yes. I mean, is there no privacy left in the world?"

"Sure there is. When you're in the ground you'll get plenty of privacy, but right now you got a roomful. Be thankful, doll." She picked up a bowl and nodded toward the other one, throwing a green dish towel over her shoulder. "Grab that and let's go. Everybody's hungry for your pasta. You should be happy I did you a favor. Rudy's back and he's in your bed. What more do you want? A special invitation? Now you can get your revenge on the louse and break your curse. You got the control. I wish that devil Pinky would come back so easy."

She winked and walked out of the kitchen. Cate picked up the other bowl and followed, wondering if Aunt Flo's people-management skills couldn't be put to better use at the UN, or even divorce court.

CATE MANAGED TO BREAK AWAY from the group to bring Rudy a plate of pasta. She carried it up on a tray, along with a few slices of bread and a glass of red wine.

When she stepped into the room, he was lying on his side, apparently fast asleep. The sight of him contentedly sleeping in the middle of her bed brought back way too many memories. She immediately knew this had been a bad idea. She should have let him go to the hospital.

"You can't sleep here," Cate said. "You have to go back to Rudyworld."

No response. He didn't budge. Rudy Bellafini was fast asleep in Cate Falco's bed.

Or was he?

She put the tray down on the nightstand.

"I know you can hear me. You can't sleep here. Everybody will start talking, teasing, and you know how this neighborhood is. One of them will call the *Times* and I'll get caught up in your scandal. I don't want it. Wake up, Rudy. Come on." She knelt on the bed to get closer to him and gave him a nudge, but he didn't move.

The man always could sleep through anything.

She reached out to nudge him again, but then pulled back when she looked at his face. God, how she had loved that face of his—those beautiful curled eyelashes, that strong chin with the slight dimple right in the middle. Most people didn't notice his dimple, but she did. She could always tell when he was stretching the truth or trying to backpedal out of some mess he'd gotten himself into. His dimple would suddenly appear. It was his silly dimple that had attracted her in the first place.

She gently touched his chin, then moved his hair off his forehead. He had such gorgeous hair, dark and rich with auburn highlights.

He moved and reached out for her. She wanted to pull away but didn't. There was a part of her that was still totally attracted to him, like a deer in his headlights.

She slid down on her side of the bed, facing him. He pulled her in tight, tighter, holding her against his muscled body. He felt warm against her body, warm and comfortable. Too comfortable. They always did fit together like they were made for each other. All the pieces fit like they were supposed to. Like God himself had planned their bodies for each other and no one else. She could feel his sleepy breath on her neck. The sensation made her skin tingle and her eyes water. She tried to move away.

He dreamily opened his eyes and kissed her.

She returned the kiss gently. His lips felt hot against hers, just the way she had remembered them. Then she kissed him with all the passion she had stored up for the past ten years. Could she let herself fall all over again for the man who had left her brokenhearted?

She pulled out of the kiss and looked into his eyes, searching for his love, but it wasn't there. He blinked a few times and said, "Turn the light out, Allison. I want to sleep." Then his eyes closed and his breathing took on an even rhythm.

Allison!

Some things never change.

There she was swooning over perfect fits and sexy dimples while he thought she was the woman who had caused all his physical pain in the first place.

Rudy Bellafini was back all right, but not for her love—for her therapy. It was as if he had planned to get caught in the back seat of her VW just to win her sympathy, and big sucker Cate was falling for it.

She turned on every light in the room and walked out slamming the door behind her, then stomped down the stairs in search of Aunt Flo. It was time to end this curse once and for all.

6

AFTER EVERYONE had gone home, Cate left with Aunt Flo. Her condo, in University Village, was only a short bus ride up Taylor Street. Flo had purchased the tiny condo two years ago, when the prices were reasonable. The condo had since almost doubled in price, and Aunt Flo considered the profit her burial money, *So I don't gotta worry about the burden of my dead body.*

Cate and Aunt Flo sat across from each other at the kitchen table. They each had a full glass of red wine in front of them, and the women had changed into red velvet gowns with matching hats.

The hats were carefully trimmed with various Italian amulets: horns, clutched hands and fresh heads of garlic. Cate had a hard time actually seeing between all the stuff dangling in her face.

Three bottles of red wine sat in the middle of the table, one was uncorked and the other two waited to be opened.

"Do you love him?" Aunt Flo asked.

"Absolutely not."

"Good. It makes things much easier. If you love him, that will make it harder to break the curse. You'll have to take a third step, and that's a hard one. This way there's only two steps."

"Then this curse-breaking should be a cinch, because I don't love him and never will."

Aunt Flo gave her a dismissive look. "Don't count your chickens."

"Just tell me what I have to do." Cate took a couple gulps of wine. Aunt Flo took more than a couple gulps, she knocked off the whole glass. Cate watched in awe. When Aunt Flo put the empty glass down on the table, Cate said, "You're pretty good at that."

"It's medicinal."

Cate finished off her own glass and poured herself another. "I feel better already."

Cate thought the wine tasted smooth and creamy, unlike any wine she had ever had. Aunt Flo uncorked another bottle, filled her own glass and carefully placed the bottle in the center of the table.

"Shall we get serious?" Aunt Flo asked.

"Serious is my middle name."

"Now we're getting somewhere, doll. What I have to tell you only makes sense when you're drunk on Sicilian wine."

Cate looked up and took a few more swigs. Her aunt displayed the bottle with both hands so that the Sicilian label gleamed under the kitchen light.

"What I'm about to tell you can only be passed down from one cursed woman to another cursed woman. It's very important that you keep this information away from the cursing man or it won't work."

Cate was slightly confused. "You mean I can't tell Rudy?"

"Right. You can't tell him a thing or the curse will never be broken, ever."

"Okay, I agree. Do I have to sign anything in blood?"

"Don't kid."

"Sorry."

Aunt Flo placed the bottle back in the center of the table. "Turn off the light and take your seat," she ordered.

As soon as Cate hit the light switch, a weird glow appeared from under the wine bottles.

"Listen closely, for I can only tell you this once."

Cate leaned in.

Aunt Flo finished off her glass of wine and poured another. Then, with a strange, faraway look in her eyes, like she was in a trance, she said, "In order for the curse to be broken, you must take certain steps to get your revenge. First, get Rudy to agree to marry you."

"Marry me?"

Aunt Flo came out of her trance. "Don't ask questions, you'll break my trance." She drank down more wine, then closed her eyes again and moaned some kind of tune. Cate thought it was Peggy Lee's "Fever," but she couldn't be sure.

"So, how do I do this?" Cate whispered.

Aunt Flo's eye's flew wide open. "Do I gotta draw you a road map to the church or what?"

Cate blushed, drank more wine and hummed "Fever."

"What's that noise?" Aunt Flo asked, while keeping her eyes closed.

"I'm chanting," Cate answered.

"Only one person can chant."

"Why?"

"Because that's the way these things are done! Do I gotta teach you everything?" Aunt Flo sounded angry.

Cate backed off. "Sorry," she said, and snapped her eyes shut.

"Let's go on," Aunt Flo ordered, and reached across

the table for Cate's hands. She chanted a little more, then stopped.

Cate waited, then felt Aunt Flo's hands on hers.

She waited some more, peeking at Aunt Flo every now and then to see if she was still awake. Then, after what seemed like ten minutes, Aunt Flo said, "The second thing you have to do, and this is important, you gotta get him to fall in love with you."

Cate opened her eyes. "But wouldn't he already be in love with me once he agrees to marry me?"

"Not necessarily. Who knows why a man gets married?"

"This is going to be tough."

"Did I ever say it would be easy? Nothing in life that's worth anything is easy. That's only in them fairy tales."

"I was just thinking—"

"Don't think. You'll get into trouble if you think too much. You gotta get your revenge. It's the only thing that will break the curse. Oh, and try not to have any...you know. It just muddles things."

Cate pulled her hands away from Aunt Flo to knock off her latest glass of wine then poured herself another one. The wine was actually numbing her need for sex. That was it, she thought. Every time she had a sex urge, she would simply drink the pesky impulse away.

"Who needs sex, anyway? It's just a distraction."

Aunt Flo opened her eyes. "Doll, when a young girl like you thinks sex is a distraction, you gotta break this curse fast, before you turn into one of them professional mourners."

"You mean like the Crying Lady at Henry's Funeral Home?"

"You think she cries for dead strangers?"

"You're right. I have to work fast. Is there anything else?" Cate asked as she sucked up more of the mind-numbing liquid. She was getting really woozy now and wanted Aunt Flo to wrap this thing up quickly, while she could still concentrate.

"Yes, everybody's gotta know that you jilted him."

"That's the easy part."

"One more thing, doll."

"I'll do anything. Tell me what it is."

Aunt Flo closed her eyes and chanted. This time she hummed until she got to the chorus and stopped. Like the word *fever* sparked something.

"By the way, if the sex part happens, try not to enjoy it." Aunt Flo opened her eyes and winked.

Cate blushed again. "So, what's the final step?"

"The woman can't take up with this man again unless she gets a sign."

"Why would she want to take up with him?"

"It happens all the time. The man who jilts is usually the one they first loved."

"What sign?"

"The woman will know when she sees it."

Aunt Flo stood up and turned the lights back on. Cate's eyes stung from the glare, plus she was now so light-headed from all the wine, she could barely see straight.

"I'm gonna get up early tomorrow, so I'll sleep in my recliner. You can have my bed." She yawned and stretched. "It's been a long day. Good night." She walked out of the room.

Cate stood and tried to focus on her aunt, but the kitchen spun in tight circles. She sat back down, folded her arms on the table, cradled her head in the center, and fell asleep under her hat of amulets and garlic.

RUDY COULD HARDLY MOVE when he awoke in Cate's bed. Every muscle in his entire body ached, and his ankle was swollen to the size of a good-size football.

So much for chivalry.

His head pounded with each beat of his heart, and if he moved too quickly nausea welled up from his stomach, probably from that plate of pasta he had eaten in the middle of the night. It forced him to lie back and rethink his feeble attempt at getting out of bed—her bed.

How the hell did I end up here?

Not that he had some sort of memory lapse and couldn't remember. He knew exactly how he had gotten there—thanks to a certain Vinney McCally. It was more a question of disbelief rather than an actual question of physics.

Matter of fact, it was a great place to be—considering that kiss he had stolen in the middle of the night. The sheets smelled of Cate, the pillow, the blankets. The entire room brought back a rush of memories he hadn't thought of in years. He knew something was up with her from the way she'd responded to his advances. Sure, he'd been a little groggy with sleep, but he'd known exactly what he was doing and he'd liked it. He'd liked the way she'd slid in close to his body. The warmth of her. The feel. Her scent.

But he remembered something else, something about Allison, but he assured himself that it must have been a dream...a bad dream. He pushed the evil thought aside. He wanted to concentrate on Cate.

He turned on his side. It took every ounce of strength

to move his arm, then his back and slide his butt around. The thought of somehow pulling himself out of bed and standing was more than he wanted to endure.

Cate walked in carrying a tray with a rose in a white vase. "Good morning, sleepyhead. I didn't want to wake you, but it's almost noon and I thought if we were going to get started on your therapy you'd need a hearty breakfast."

She put the tray down on the bed, walked over to the window, spread the curtains apart and opened the window, wide. "Ah, smell that clean air." She took in a deep breath. "There's nothing like it after a night of snow and sleet. It washes everything clean. Don't you think?"

He smiled, but the breeze was bitter cold. He pulled the blankets up on his chest.

"I made you a couple scrambled eggs, whole-grain toast with honey, a bowl of Optimum cereal, some green tea and freshly squeezed orange juice. Oh, and there's a cup of vitamins to get you going."

She looked amazing, tight, cropped sweater, low-cut jeans. She even had a belly-button ring, and he loved belly-button rings.

"A cup of vitamins...I don't know that—"

"A person can never have too many vitamins. It's what keeps our bodies healthy. Strong. Vibrant."

"I don't know about vibrant, but—"

"I've got our day all planned out. I've gone over your medical records—thank you for leaving them on my desk by the way—and it's crystal clear what course I have to take. You need aggressive treatment so that when you return to the slopes you'll be stronger and in better shape than you were when the injuries occurred."

With the way Rudy felt, the words *aggressive* and *treatment* shouldn't be in the same sentence. "You think we could take this healing thing a little slower? You're starting to scare me."

"Poor baby. Don't be scared. Catie won't hurt you, well, at least I won't do it on purpose. No pain, no gain. You of all people should know that," she smiled, and walked to his bedside. She leaned over. He flinched, expecting the worse, but she reached for his pillow. "Here, let me make you more comfortable."

He was beginning to like this: Cate Falco waiting on him, making him breakfast; her tight sweater. She fluffed his pillow and helped to get him situated on the bed.

"As soon as you finish your breakfast, I'll need to give you a complete physical to find out the level of your mobility. I want a total understanding of your injuries before I can stabilize you and come up with an effective treatment."

He relaxed.

She winked.

Cate Falco actually winked. Was she flirting?

The girl must have come to her senses and realized there was no reason to be mad at him. He didn't have to apologize for walking out on her after all. She seemed fine with everything now. He figured maybe it was that kiss last night and decided to test his theory.

"Cate, about last night. About that kiss—"

"I'm sorry about that. I forgot myself for a minute...you know how attractive you are. I'll try to behave from now on," she said.

Rudy was in shock. Cate Falco, the girl he had been nervous about seeing again, was apologizing for kissing him in the middle of the night. This was very good. Very good indeed.

She sat down on the bed. "So, do you want me to feed you or can you manage?"

He thought this was just too awesome, and he may as well go with it. "Well, I do feel a little weak this morning."

She picked up a fork, scooped up a mound of eggs and said, "Open wide, honey, cause I'm coming through."

7

CATE SPENT the next two days working on Rudy's various ailments and honing her wooing skills. She hadn't been this sweet to a guy, well, ever. He seemed to be lapping it up in perfect Rudy fashion.

The clinic was closed on Sundays and Mondays so she had plenty of time to concentrate on him. She treated Rudy like any other athlete with injuries. His injuries were the least of her problems. It was his ego that required the hard work.

By early Monday evening she was exhausted. All that smiling and flirting was getting to her. She concluded that wooing was entirely too much effort, especially when it was fake wooing. It was a good thing she had a fashion-conscious sister to help with clothes and jewelry, and hip dating secrets or she'd be hopeless.

The only good thing about it all was that Rudy, with his self-absorbed self, was completely and blissfully clueless.

Cate had made the decision to let him stay in her bed, for now, and hoped any lurking paparazzi would get tired of the wait and leave them alone.

A timer went off in the kitchen, and Cate was just getting ready to pull a roasted chicken out of the oven that Gina had made, when Rudy walked in, dressed in black slacks and a black shirt. He looked marvelous, despite his crutches.

"Thanks for the clothes. They fit perfectly," he said.

"I'm so glad. I wasn't sure about the size. Your chest has gotten *so* muscular."

He stuck out his chest like a peacock showing off its feathers. "Let's go out for dinner. Just you and me," he said as he swung himself closer to her. Apparently, all the physical therapy had helped. He was able to move around quite easily.

"Are you sure you're up for it? We can stay right here. Gina baked a chicken. My dad likes chicken and penne pasta on Monday nights. Wouldn't you like a nice home-cooked meal with my family?"

Cate leaned over, purposely sticking her butt out a little, not too much, just enough to make him drool, and pulled the perfectly roasted chicken out of the oven. It smelled and looked delicious surrounded with carrots, onions and red potatoes, just as it did every Monday night...that was the problem. There had been too many Monday-night chickens lately, and Cate longed for a break, even if it was with Rudy Bellafini.

"So, let them eat chicken. Come on. I want to buy you a great meal. It's the least I can do."

"But you shouldn't put any pressure on that foot." That was the truth. Even though she was playing with his emotions, she was serious about his injuries.

"I'm not running a marathon. I'm eating dinner. I'll be sitting down the whole time."

"I'll be ready in ten minutes." She probably could have done it in five, but she didn't want to seem too anxious.

"Then it's a date," he said, sneaking a baby carrot out of the pan.

"Last chance." She held up a massive piece of foil.

"No, thanks. I think it's time for us to get out of here."

She covered the Monday-night chicken and left it on the stove. Rudy headed out to the other room to wait.

Cate had a hard time believing that her plan was working so quickly and so easily. She had spent years resenting him for causing her so much pain, not to mention all the pain her boyfriends had had to endure, and all she had to do was show him some skin and flirt a little and he turned into putty.

But she told herself to calm down. They weren't standing at the altar yet, matter of fact they were a long way from the altar, but at least they were headed up the right aisle.

Somewhere in the back of her mind she always knew why he had left, and why she wouldn't have gone with him, but it was the way he did it. Not even a phone call, or a note, or a damn message on her answering machine. Nothing but silence.

And everything had happened so fast, Rudy's proposal, her scholarship to UCLA, his acceptance with that ski coach. At the time she'd had some doubts about the marriage, and thought he did, too. They each had dreams to fulfill and marriage would just get in their way. She was even thinking about postponing it, but that's when he'd disappeared.

It was the day after they had decided on a wedding date. She had made an appointment with Father Joe at Saint Mary's to finalize everything, and Rudy hadn't shown up. She'd been late, way late, and thought he'd gotten angry and gone back home. She walked over to his house to try and sort things out, but he wasn't there. His mother invited Cate in, poured two cups of strong coffee and told Cate that he'd packed up his stuff and left for Colorado on a 7:00 a.m. flight. It took several cups of coffee for Cate to realize that he wasn't coming back.

She had to admit that, at the time, there was a small part of her that was happy he'd gone, but when he never phoned and weird stuff started happening to her subsequent boyfriends, she began to resent him more and more.

Okay, she was getting angry again, and the one thing she didn't want for dinner was a plate of anger. How could she get him to trust her and fall in love with her if she was angry? She closed her eyes and took a couple of deep, cleansing breaths to let it go.

They worked nicely.

Cate ran a comb through her hair, sprayed on Giorgio's "So You," and slipped on a hot little number—a black, knee-length sheath with cleavage. She pulled on pantyhose and stepped into a pair of Gina's bronze-colored heels.

Cate had been so busy working that she had almost given up on chi-chi shoes and funky clothes. It felt incredibly good to slide her feet into a pair of really high and pointy heels for that crunched-up-toe effect.

A real style rush.

Cate was fabulously ready in eight minutes flat.

CATE OPENED THE FRONT DOOR of Carmen's Side Room where a big guy with thick, black hair, wearing a black suit, greeted her. "Ah, Cate Falco, it's been a long time."

They hugged. He smelled of sweet cologne. She told him about how the paparazzi had followed her and Rudy Bellafini to the restaurant.

"*The* Rudy Bellafini...the gold medalist?" Carmen turned his attention to Rudy.

"Yep."

Carmen grabbed Rudy and gave him a kiss on each cheek along with a great big bear hug.

"You honor me. Come, sit down. The boys and me will take care of everything."

In no less than fifteen minutes she and Rudy were seated at an intimate corner table of the crowded little restaurant and a good-looking waiter with green eyes, brown hair and a thick Italian accent was pouring two glasses of red wine.

Rudy said, "You're amazing."

She smiled and answered, "I know," but she was actually shaking on the inside. Even though she had been in complete control over the car, she had never driven that fast or that crazy in her entire life. It had been a real adrenaline rush.

He laughed and reached for her hand.

And so we begin, she thought as they held hands for a moment across the table.

Rudy glanced around the room. "Half the people in this place look like they belong to the mob."

There was a group of guys standing at the bar. One of them, a rather large guy in a gray silk suit had slicked-back hair and a bulldog face. Another taller guy wore a bunch of gold necklaces and rings on every finger. Then there was the older man with Elvis Presley hair. He was the best. He even wore the signature gold-rimmed Elvis shades.

"It was the only place I could think of where I knew we'd be safe. Nobody gets in here who isn't welcome."

"And you're welcome?"

"I worked on Carmen Petrassi, the guy standing at the bar. The one who looks like Elvis. He had a hamstring problem."

"You mean the guy who's coming over?"

Carmen walked straight to their table, bowed a little, straightened his red silk tie and said, "Cate, you honor me by bringing such a champion to my establishment."

Cate did the introductions, Rudy stood, and the two men shook hands. "Do not worry about a thing, my friend. No one will bother you for the rest of the evening. Relax. Enjoy yourselves. I'm sending over another bottle of wine. My compliments."

"Thank you," Cate said. He kissed her hand and walked away.

"Like I said before, you're amazing," Rudy said.

Cate took another sip of her wine and threw him a coy smile. Just keep reeling him in, she thought, a little at a time.

They sat in a wooden booth with a white linen tablecloth, surrounded by low lighting and old Chicago ambiance. An autographed picture of Frank Sinatra stared down at them while a guy in his late forties, standing on a tiny stage at the other end of the room, sang Dean Martin's "That's Amore," from the movie *Moonstruck*.

After Rudy finished off his first glass of Chianti, and all the small talk about the restaurant and the neighborhood ended, and after they ordered their meal, he said, "I want to thank you for letting me stay in your house and taking such good care of me, Cate. You still have that..." He hesitated.

"You can say it."

"You still have that magic touch."

"You're welcome," she answered. "You've been a good patient."

There were a few people dancing up by the stage. "I love to dance, especially to something nice and slow," he said. "I remember that I could never get you out on a dance floor, and now I really can't."

"I'm still a klutz. Never learned."

"Too bad. There's nothing as sexy as cuddling on a dance floor."

Cate, now completely relaxed, and feeling proud of herself for the drive and getting through the last couple days, casually glanced around the room. A woman caught her eye sitting at a corner table, next to the stage, laughing and holding hands with his companion. Cate turned so she could get a better look at the woman dressed entirely in gold, and sure enough it was Aunt Flo and some man. She couldn't quite make out who the guy was because he was hidden by an older couple on the dance floor.

"Oh, my God!" Cate said covering her mouth with her hand. *Of all the places in Chicago to come to hide, I had to pick this one.*

"Isn't that your dad over there?" Rudy asked, nodding toward Aunt Flo's table.

"My dad! No. It's not my dad. He's home eating chicken. Aunt Flo is out with some guy I've never seen before, not with my dad. He doesn't come out to places like this. He's very methodical. Set in his ways. He wouldn't be caught dead out here on a Monday night. No. It's not my dad. My aunt Flo, maybe, but not my dad."

"I think you're wrong, Cate. It's your dad *and* Aunt Flo, and from the looks of it, I'd say those two are getting it on."

"Oh, please," Cate said. The whole concept of her father and Aunt Flo getting it on was totally out of the question. Aunt Flo was too flamboyant and eccentric, and her dad was so...her dad. He didn't get it on...at least not anymore. She didn't want to even think about it.

"No. Really. Look at them, all cozy, sitting at a dark table, holding hands, laughing. And why this place? I'm telling you, Cate. He's getting a little, and they don't want anybody to know."

"Stop it! That's sick. That's my dad you're talking about." Wasn't it enough that Rudy was back in her life? Did she now have to stress over her dad and Aunt Flo having some secret affair?

"If you don't believe me, check it out for yourself. Do it now. They're not looking."

Cate turned around to get a better look just as her father reached over and touched Aunt Flo's cheek. She nearly fell off her bench seat. It was one thing to see them together in a restaurant and speculate on a possible affair, but it was quite another thing to actually see them physically touch.

Cate's chest started to tighten.

Rudy said, "How long have they been an item?"

Cate turned on Rudy. "My father's not the item type. They're just having dinner, that's all."

"They're having more than dinner."

Cate snuck another peek and sure enough, her dad was looking all mushy at Aunt Flo. The whole idea was more than she could imagine. "I have to get out of here. Can we please leave?"

"I don't think Carmen would be too happy if we left before the main course, besides I think they're leaving. They're coming this way."

"This isn't right. Not my aunt. She's too old. And he's even older."

Cate slid over to the wall, and held up her napkin trying to hide behind it. If she could, she would have slid under the table. She actually considered it for a moment, but then regained her sanity. She held up a tiny dessert menu instead. Rudy did the same thing, only he tried to have a conversation while they hid.

"Why are we hiding?"

"I don't want them to see us," she whispered.

"Why?"

"I don't know. Yes, I do. They'll want to talk, or worse, explain. I don't want to hear it. Not now. Not while I'm still coping. It's too weird. Tell me when they're gone, but don't let them see you."

Rudy peeked over his menu. "They're talking to some of the guys at the bar."

"Damn!"

"Don't panic. Everybody's shaking hands. More hand shaking. Smiling, a lot of smiling. Okay, now they're leaving."

"Are you sure?"

"Yes, they're walking out. He put his arm around her waist."

"I don't need the details, thank you."

"Then you don't want to know about their kiss?"

"Oh, my God! No. I don't want to know about their kiss." But Cate couldn't stop herself. She had to look. Sure enough, there was Pinky-cursed Aunt Flo and set-in-his-ways Dad stealing a kiss while they slipped on their coats. It wasn't a long kiss, just a simple smooch, but it was a lip lock nonetheless. Then he took her hand and they strolled out the front door.

Cate leaned sideways and sprawled herself across the bench seat in a tension release. The waiter arrived with their meal. "Are you all right, *signorina?*" he asked as he placed a plate of steaming baked ziti on the table in front of her.

"Sure. I'm fine. Just fine," she said looking up at him from the seat.

"Do you need anything?"

"A normal life."

"But we are Italian."

"Thank you for reminding me."

"You are welcome. Now, please. The ziti will get cold, and Carmen will blame me if you do not like your dinner."

She sat up, picked up her fork and took a bite. The flavors exploded in her mouth. "Tell Carmen his ziti are perfect."

The waiter smiled and left, then she and Rudy started laughing, and continued to laugh and talk as if they had never been apart.

8

THE DRIVE HOME was slow and peaceful, thanks to Carmen's escort service. Cate's Lexus was surrounded by black Caddies. There were no cars chasing them or photo-crazed madmen trying to make a buck off of somebody else's private life.

By the time Cate and Rudy walked up to her back door, she had Rudy primed and ready for her first real kiss.

"Look at all those stars," Rudy said gazing up at the night sky. "I don't remember all those stars."

"You don't?"

"No."

He moved in closer.

"Do you remember this?" she asked. They were staring at each other now. Cate tilted her head, and Rudy moved in for the kiss.

It started slow and easy, Cate trying to keep it light but needing him to want more. His lips felt amazingly warm and luscious, and when his tongue gently brushed her lips, she knew it was all over for him. He was hers for the taking.

He slowly pulled out of the kiss, gazed into her eyes for a moment, smiled, and was just about to kiss her again when she moved away.

Rudy just about fell over. She caught him, and he regained his balance.

"It's getting late. We better go inside and get you into bed so we can have an early start."

She couldn't do it. Not yet. She wasn't ready to make real lip and tongue contact with Rudy. Kissing was such a personal thing. Such a love moment, and she wasn't quite ready for faking her love moment, not after they'd had such a nice evening. Besides, he needed more priming. He'd want her even more after this little episode.

"But Cate, I—"

She opened the door with her key and walked inside. Rudy followed as she snapped on the kitchen light. It stung her eyes.

"Well then, I'll see you in the morning," she told him, and left him standing in the kitchen as she made her way up to Gina's bedroom.

CATE COULDN'T SLEEP. *Christ, he's beautiful. Going to be a big problem. Get over it.*

Finally, sick of tossing and turning, playing games with herself about this guy, she woke up Gina. They lay across from each other, on opposite sides of the bed, resting on pillows in the dark. They could see each other courtesy of Gina's Bugs Bunny nightlight. "But did you kiss him back?" Gina asked.

"I didn't have a choice. His lips were right there," Cate answered, trying to justify her emotions.

"And did you like it?"

"That's the problem. I kinda did." Cate didn't want to admit that she was actually afraid of what might happen with another kiss.

"This is so not cool, Cate. You're going to fall for him again. Don't forget what happened to Paul Leoni."

"Oh, Paul." She sighed. "He was pretty and that's always a problem for me. I need to go ugly." She had really fallen for Paul. He had such a great smile and loved to dance. Paul was a fabulous dancer, especially to something slow. He knew how to hold a woman in his arms. She felt herself flush just thinking about him.

"Yeah, well, wasn't he stuck in a revolving door for, like, two hours in some candy store?"

"Fannie May, and it was three hours."

"On your second date?"

"Technically, it was our first." She remembered how confused he looked standing in between the glass doors, holding his little white bag of chocolate Pixies while an assortment of rescue workers tried to figure out how to get him out of there.

"And who was that guy out in California who kept getting his car stolen?"

Cate had all but forgotten about Brian, the design engineer.

"He didn't count. Brian kept parking in strange places."

"Oh!"

"That's not what I mean," Cate said.

"Yeah, like in front of your apartment."

"It was a tough neighborhood."

"Cate, you lived on campus."

"It was a tough campus."

Brian would park his car, walk up the stairs for Cate, they'd make small talk while she collected her things, then they'd walk back outside, and his car would be missing. She actually never got to go anywhere with him, but she did get to know the local cops fairly well.

"You made your point. No I'm not going to fall for

Rudy again. Even if I did, it wouldn't matter. I don't have any choice. I have to break this stupid curse," she said, and immediately felt stronger for having said it.

I'm going to get my revenge. Break my curse. Revenge!

"Just be careful with that stuff. Revenge can get ugly." Gina punched her pillow and slipped down lower on the bed.

Cate stopped her mantra. Gina was right. She had to be more cautious about this whole thing.

"Not if I do it right. Not if I do what Aunt Flo told me to do."

"You really believe her about all this, don't you?"

"Not in the beginning, I didn't. Not until I got the proof from everybody I dated. One accident is an accident. Two is bad luck. Three is a definite pattern, and definite patterns are caused by something."

Cate snuggled farther down, as well, and pulled the flannel sheets and blankets up around her shoulders. Gina liked to keep her room as cold as possible at night. She slept in sweats, socks and fingerless gloves. Cate slept in silk pajamas.

"Aunt Flo? I suppose she told you in order to break your curse you have to kiss Rudy? Is he going to turn into a total prince and whisk you away to some castle?"

"Nothing that simple. Actually, she told me I have get Rudy to propose to me."

"Oh. Is that all?"

Cate was hesitant about telling Gina the second part of the curse breaker. It sounded somewhat easy to do when she was drunk on Sicilian wine, with Aunt Flo chanting "Fever," but now, well, she wasn't so sure of herself.

"And he has to be in love with me. It's the only way to break this thing."

Gina stared at Cate. "How are you ever going to pull that one off, if you can't even handle a little kiss?"

She might have a point, Cate thought. "I've had a long time to get strong. But if I do look like I'm weakening, I need you to remind me what I'm doing. This time, I'm the flame and he's the moth."

"We'll see who gets burned," Gina said skeptically as she cradled her pillow.

"Will you keep reminding me?" Cate figured she was going to need all the help she could get. Rationally she knew what she had to do, but she wasn't so sure she could handle the emotional part.

"You're really going to do this, aren't you?" Her eyes were closing.

"Yes. I don't have any other choice. He's never been loyal to any woman in his entire life and never will be. I just have to keep telling myself that I'm only using him to break my curse. Nothing more."

"Then get some sleep. You've got a lot of toad kissing to do."

Cate started to get comfortable, then remembered that she forgot to tell Gina about Aunt Flo and their dad. "Remind me to tell you about Dad tomorrow. You won't believe what I saw."

But Gina was already sound asleep.

BY EIGHT-THIRTY the next morning Rudy felt as if he was back online and in charge of his life once again. The paparazzi were nowhere in sight, so he insisted they drive over to Cate's Wellness Center instead of giving him yet another treatment at home.

Ever since the lift incident, he had taken himself out of the business game, but now that Cate had worked on the physical, the mental had returned with even more clarity.

His business was in need of its leader, and he finally felt up to the challenge.

While he worked his legs on the recumbent bike, Rudy ordered a revamp of all his Tomato Garden menus. "I want a new base tomato sauce," he said into his cell phone. Compared to Cate's simple pasta sauce, his sauces reeked. "And I want my best chefs in charge of this with a final taste-off next Sunday in my Chicago restaurant."

During whirlpool therapy, he put together a construction crew to remodel the brownstone and made sure the Volkswagen had someone working on it around the clock.

That in itself was a challenge. No one ever seemed to answer the phone at Ted's Body Shop, and even though Ted had assured him that the car was being worked on, after seeing him with Aunt Flo, Rudy couldn't be sure that Ted had room for anything else but his new love life.

After Cate hooked him up to the muscle stimulator, Rudy ordered a couple Nautilus machines for the Wellness Center, but didn't exactly know what else she needed, so he left it up to the salesman to contact Cate for the details.

During all this activity, he found himself lingering over the very idea of Cate Falco. He had always thought of her as an incredible chick, with a tight body and a killer sense of humor, but he never thought of Cate as edgy. But after that dinner last night, surrounded by all those mob types, he'd have to reconsider.

She'd handled the paparazzi on the way to the restaurant and she'd driven to the one place where she and Rudy were assured of privacy. The woman had completely taken him by surprise.

He watched as she talked to other patients at the center and as she helped someone with an exercise or showed another therapist how to work a machine. She moved with self-confidence and authority, and every so often she'd look over and throw him one of her smiles. It gave him a rush every time.

CATE SLOWLY MASSAGED his shoulders, digging her thumbs into his scapula as she had done several times before, but this time it sent his heart racing and his emotions swirling. The cell phone he still clutched in his hand rang.

He didn't recognize the number that flashed up on the tiny screen, but thought it might be important so he answered. "Hello," he said into the phone.

"It's me, you devil, you. Where have you been?" Allison cooed into his ear. His whole body tensed.

"Relax," Cate urged.

He hadn't returned any of Allison's phone calls, and each time she had called he wouldn't answer.

"Hibernating in the cold," he said, wanting to get rid of her. He thought of just hitting the disconnect button, but he knew Allison well enough to know she would just call back.

"You can at least tell me where you're hiding so I can make up to you in person. I know I've been a bad girl, but all that's changed now. I've joined an anger management group. Dr. Moray says I'm his best patient. Please let me prove it to you, sugar. I don't know how I can go on another minute without seeing you again. Besides, Dr. Moray says you're part of my cure. You do want me to be cured, don't you?" Allison whimpered. He'd forgotten how manipulative she could be.

Cate ran her hands along the sides of his back. It felt incredible, and he wanted to let out a moan, but Allison was listening.

"That's not possible," he said, definitely not wanting her to show up on Cate's doorstep.

"But I'm so very sorry, sugar. Can't we start over? Anyway, I don't think it was my fault you fell. The chair was defective."

"Come on, let's be real." Rudy wasn't in the mood for her. He'd had a good day and didn't want anything to spoil it, but he was beginning to feel his neck tighten.

"But you know how much I love you, sugar. I would *never* do anything to hurt you."

Cate whispered in his other ear, "Maybe you should tell whoever it is to go away. I need you to focus on me." Her breath was warm and it tickled his ear.

"I know," he said to Cate.

"Good, then tell me where you are, sugar. Showing is so much better than telling."

Allison had turned out to be a little more high-maintenance and high-strung than he could deal with. But getting away from her was proving to be as difficult as being with her. Her charms, and they were many, all led to control. If she could control the weather and the Middle East, she would. Without even thinking about it, he let out a small moan, and as soon as he did, he realized that Allison would think it was because of her.

He still wondered if that little nudge that had thrown him off the chair lift was an accident, as she claimed, or deliberate. He'd been trying to break off with her, and she wasn't taking it well. Next time he'd have his feet firmly on the ground.

"Look, I'll call you after a few more days of therapy, when I'm feeling better. I've got to go." He had no intention of calling her, but it was the only way to get her to stop bugging him.

"But you can't go. I haven't told you my surprise yet."

He tried to remain calm, but knowing Allison, the surprise probably had something to do with the media. "I don't like surprises."

"Oh, but this is fabulous news!"

Whatever it was, Rudy didn't want to hear it during a massage with Cate. "I'll call you later." He hung up and pressed the power button on his cell so she couldn't call back.

"How was that?" Cate asked after she finished his massage.

"Great. Can we talk?" He wanted to clear things up with Cate, apologize. He'd never meant to hurt her. He was young and stupid and didn't know a good thing when it was right in front of him.

CATE WIPED THE LOTION from her hands on a clean white towel, wondering what he could possibly want to talk about. She saw his hand reaching out toward her.

"Talk about what?" She backed off.

"I never got a chance—"

"The past is what it is. I'd as soon not open old wounds, if you don't mind. I want to work on that hip of yours. I'll be right back with a heating pad."

She walked out of the room and continued on out the front door. She needed air. *Great*, she thought, *what's he think, that he can waltz in here and say he's sorry! Give me a break.*

The cold air felt especially good on her hot skin. She took a couple of deep breaths, paced for a few minutes, trying to regain her control.

She could feel the sexual tension building inside her, and she knew he could feel it, as well, which was a good thing, but she was losing control. Losing focus. She wasn't going to succumb to this guy's charms again. No way in hell. But even if she did, she wouldn't follow her heart. Whoever told little girls to follow their heart was a sadist or a fool.

That moan gave him away. He was ready. If she played him right, she could probably get some kind of commitment out of him any day now. The whole thing made her shake. Or was it the cold?

She stopped pacing, threw her shoulders back and marched into the building, feeling slightly foolish for ever having *Rudy* and *erotic* in the same thought.

"WHAT DO YOU MEAN she's on her way over here?" Rudy was talking to the head of the construction crew renovating his house as he paced in Cate's bedroom.

"She showed up here and asked where you were. So I told her. You didn't say—"

"Don't worry about it."

After hanging up, Rudy walked over to the window,

and there she was, dancing across the street in that peculiar way she had. Somewhere between walking, skipping and flying. And the damn paparazzi trailing like a pack of wild dogs. This is just great, he thought.

He turned from the window and walked to his open door. He heard her down on the landing talking to Gina. Next thing he knew, she was bounding up the steps like a show poodle.

Allison stormed in, all bright and shiny, but a pall came over her as she looked around the room. "Why are you staying here?"

"My house is being—"

"I know, but why aren't you at a hotel?"

"Well, I figured since my therapy—"

"This is a woman's bedroom! Whose bedroom is this?"

"Well, it's...it doesn't matter as long as—"

"Oh? You're in some woman's bedroom and it's not mine. Doesn't look like mine. I hate this look, by the way. It's really low class. And pink! God, I hate pink. It's so last year, sugar. Who is this benefactress that gave up her room to you?"

"My therapist."

"Your therapist! How old is she?"

"Allison, you came here with some kind of surprise."

"I did indeed. And I'm the one being surprised at the moment. You better not be playing games on me."

"How can I be playing games on you when we're not an item—"

"Oh, but we are a very big item. You see all those idiot paparazzi. They're here for a reason."

"What are you talking about?"

"The three of us."

"Listen, I'm not involved with Cate."

"Cate, is it? Is she the little therapist with the too-pink bedroom you're so comfortable in?"

"Yes. She's an old friend."

"How old of a friend is she?"

"That's not the point. What's this surprise? Why are you here? Can we just get to that?"

"I'm having your baby."

He staggered back a half step and thought for a moment he might either run through the door or jump out the window. But he didn't want to give the press a good shot.

"What?"

"You heard me, Daddy. I'm having your baby, and the whole world is going to know about it, because you and I, arm in arm, are going down there and announcing it. I let the word get out that I had something very big, very juicy. This is great. It'll bring both of us right back to center stage."

For a moment he couldn't speak. He stared at her, not sure what to think or say. This couldn't be. My God, no. Tell me it's not so. Look at her. She's thrilled. It's like she just won the Miss Celebrity of the Year contest.

"You...you're sure your pregnant. You know, I read about these false preg—"

"Sorry, sugar, this is the real deal."

"It's mine?"

"Of course it's yours."

"How do I know that?"

"You bastard! Don't start with that. I haven't been sleeping with anyone but you."

"We haven't slept together in months."

"Did you forget, sugar? How you got a little drunk the first night of the ski trip. Actually, a lot drunk."

He had gotten very drunk, in fact. And he couldn't remember if they'd had sex or not. "I don't remember."

"But I do."

"I don't believe you."

Now her mood swung radically. She began with that famous pout, her lips turning down, her eyes growing wide, as if she was welling up for a tear storm. He was going to get the complete Allison treatment, and he couldn't deal with that. Crying women drove him over the edge.

She started pacing, a habit she got into whenever she was trying to bully somebody. It was more like stalking than pacing, and it drove Rudy crazy. He wished she would just sit down.

She took out her cigarette case. The gold one he'd given her at the beginning of their relationship. If he couldn't get her to stop, she might as well smoke in style. Or at least that's how he rationalized her bad habit at the time.

She turned to face him and took a long drag on her ultraslim cigarette. When she let the smoke out, it hit Rudy right in the face.

He waved his hand to get rid of the lingering smoke. "You're pregnant and you're *smoking!*"

"That's because you're making me nervous. This is not what I expected. This is unacceptable. But I understand, sugar. It's how men are when they find out they're going to be a daddy for the first time. So I forgive you your panic. But——" she made a face and shook her head, pointing her cigarette right at him "—don't push me. I'm in a delicate state. So we have to get married as soon as possible. I even bought myself an engagement ring because I know how busy you are these days."

She held up her left hand and there, on her ring finger was a huge square-cut diamond. "I bought it at Tiffany's and opened an account for you."

Rudy's mind raced. This couldn't be happening. She couldn't be pregnant.

"This is the happiest moment of my life and you are not going to ruin it by playing games." Tears started to well up again.

"Don't cry. I'm just a little surprised, that's all. Are you really sure?" He reached out to comfort her but thought better of it. Instead he sat back down on the bed.

"Absolutely positive." She took a drag from her cigarette. "I took one of those little tests, at home."

"Then why are you still smoking?"

She looked at the cigarette as though she suddenly realized it was in her hand and immediately dropped it in his water glass on the nightstand. "You're right. I should quit this nasty habit once and for all. It causes premature wrinkling."

She sat him down on the bed, squeezing in next to him, while resting her head on his shoulder. "You'll adjust, sugar. Don't even think of running out on this. You do and I'll make you pay in every way there is. Believe me, you know how vindictive a jilted woman can be."

She reeked of smoke.

He didn't want the baby news to get out, at least not

before he knew for sure if it was true. He just didn't trust Allison, she was a fairly good actress, and an even better manipulator. This was a disaster. Not what he'd pictured for himself and his family. Somehow he'd thought when he did finally settle down with a woman, they'd be totally in love. He always saw himself, his wife and his baby living together in some small house, enjoying each other's company. Lately that idyllic scene had included Cate Falco, not Allison Devine.

If Allison's pregnancy was real, what choice did he have? He would never allow a child of his to be raised by her, alone. If he was a father, he'd be a father. Maybe having a baby would change her! Maybe some of her narcissism would give way to maternal hormones. Not that he believed that would really happen.

She looked up at him, a smile on her face. "See, you're beginning to relax. Look at the bright side, sugar. I'm as good as you're ever going to get. And now there'll be two of me!"

9

"THIS IS ALLISON DEVINE. Allison, this is Cate Falco, my therapist," Rudy said.

Cate was about to extend her hand, but the tall anemic-looking blonde didn't look as if she wanted to shake hands. Instead she gave Cate a quick once-over and then said curtly, "So, where do you sleep now that you were so generous as to give up your bed to my fiancé?"

The intensity of the woman caught Cate off guard. She couldn't process what this woman was saying.

"I sleep with my sister," Cate said.

Allison gave her a skeptical look, as though she didn't quite believe her.

Cate turned to Rudy. He sat in a chair in Cate's bedroom, pillows fluffed up behind his back. A black silk robe, something Cate hadn't seen before, covered his body, and Allison stood next to him holding a flute of champagne. An open bottle of Dom sat on the nightstand.

Allison held up her flute, fingers wrapped purposely around the glass so that her wide-load diamond ring couldn't be missed. "Well, anyway, Cat, it's so nice to finally meet you. Rudy's been telling me such nice things about you." She took a step toward Cate and shook her hand. "You look exactly like what I had expected."

She stepped back, letting go of Cate's hand to get a better look.

"It's Cate. Nice to meet you, too." The words came out smoothly, but Cate's brain suddenly felt muddy.

Allison spun around and took a seat on the edge of the bed close to Rudy. She took his hand. "That silly ol' chairlift must have been defective. We should sue, sugar. I could have died or something."

"Did you fall off, too?" Cate asked.

"No, but I could have. Just thinking about it makes me shiver with fright." She shuddered.

Cate mimicked Allison's shudder. "I bet it does," Cate said, sarcasm staining her voice.

"We'll be out of your *hair* in just a bit, Cat. I called for a limo." Allison leaned in and kissed Rudy on the lips. One of those "I'm now in charge" kisses. Cate couldn't help but think of that Frank Sinatra song, one of Aunt Flo's favorites, about being caught in the "tender trap."

"Let me get his things," Cate said, wanting to get out of the room. She couldn't deal with some other woman kissing Rudy.

"Oh, don't bother. I've already put them in my bag." She pointed to a rather large designer bag that perfectly matched her black tweed outfit. Allison looked as if she had just stepped off a page of *Marie Claire*, with her miniskirt, black over-the-knee boots and chic big hair. She was totally "now," and Cate was totally disgusted.

"Well then—" Cate felt completely out of place in her own bedroom. She wanted to say a few things, especially to Rudy, but none of it was appropriate for her father's house.

Rudy broke the silence. "I'll still be coming into the clinic, that is if you can fit me into your schedule."

"Anytime. I mean, it's my slow season right now, so there shouldn't be a problem getting you some appointments. Gina will set you up with a schedule."

Allison leaned over and ran a finger along Rudy's lips and down his chin. "Don't you worry about those little appointments. I'll make them, sugar. An important man like you doesn't have time for silly things like appointments. I'll take care of everything so you can focus all your energy on our company. I mean, if I'm going to be Mrs. Rudy Bellafini, and the mother of your children, I need to start doing all those wifely things."

Cate was stunned and confused. The newspaper article hadn't mentioned anything about his engagement, and neither had Rudy. The man was even a worse scoundrel than she could have imagined.

If Cate had been capable of giving this woman the evil eye, she would have, but she'd never learned the technique. She suddenly had a real need to learn, so she stared at Allison Devine. Stared right at her. She could feel her eyes getting tighter, and her forehead getting all wrinkled up.

The woman was destroying her plan.

CATE LEFT THEM to pack Rudy's clothes. The evil-eye thing hadn't worked, so she went downstairs where Gina met her at the bottom of the stairway. Behind Gina she saw Aunt Flo. Behind Aunt Flo was Henry.

"Nobody has anything better to do than listen in on other people's conversations?" Cate said with exasperation.

Gina took her aside. "Before you went up there, I heard Allison tell him she's pregnant."

Cate looked at Gina. "She's pregnant? She told him that?"

"Yes."

Flo pulled Cate into the kitchen. Gina and Henry followed. "That woman is lying through her capped teeth," Flo said. "Nothing that comes out of that Botox face has a bit of truth to it. I know her kind."

Cate and Flo sat down across from each other at the kitchen table. Henry and Gina hovered near the refrigerator.

"Well, I guess that's that," Cate said.

"You can't quit now." Aunt Flo reached across the table and took her hand. "We're just getting started. That woman's lying."

"You don't know that."

"I certainly do know that. When a woman's pregnant, she does things different without realizing it. She stops dashing across streets like some kid or racing up steps. And she doesn't drink or smoke. It's instinct. When she looks in any mirror, like that woman upstairs did, along with fixing her hair and makeup, she likes to stand sideways and check out her tummy to see if there's anything showing yet. She didn't do that part. That woman ain't pregnant. My dead cat's more pregnant than she is."

"You had a cat?"

"No, and she ain't pregnant, either."

Cate stared at Aunt Flo. "Whether the woman is lying or telling the truth the fact is Rudy believes her and they're leaving. Together."

"We can't let them leave without you giving *him* something to fret about."

"What do you mean?"

"A man's stupid with that kind of woman. I see how he looks at you. He's a man in love."

"I don't think so."

"He is. Believe me. I know these things. I see what's in his eyes. He's in your bed, and he wants you with him all the time and that ain't just for physical therapy. You got him. Now she should just take him away and that's the end of it? And you're stuck being cursed for the rest of your life?"

"I can't stop him."

"You got to make him remember what he's gonna give up when he leaves."

"How?"

Flo turned and looked at Henry, then back at Cate.

Cate said, "What?"

Flo nodded, as if coming to some great revelation. "What makes a man jealous? Another man."

"What are you talking about?" Cate asked.

Gina said, "Aunt Flo, you're a genius. Exactly."

Cate turned to Gina. "Is somebody going to tell me what you're talking about?"

Gina and Flo exchanged looks. Aunt Flo and Gina both turned then and looked at Henry.

Henry said, "What?"

"You," Aunt Flo ordered, "have proposed to this young lady several times and always got a no. So, what you're going to do right this minute is propose...again. Get down on your knee."

"What's going on?" Henry said, flustered.

Gina said, "Get that ring out you carry around in

your pocket, Henry O'Toole. You are about to propose to my sister."

"What! What...I...this..."

"This is ridiculous," Cate said. "Henry, don't listen to them."

Aunt Flo got a stern look on her face. "Henry, I know things about you and your Crying Lady, so don't you be playing any games. We need you. Cate needs you if she's ever gonna break the curse."

"But it's not a real proposal she'd be accepting!" Henry protested.

"Maybe not. But it's a definite step in the right direction. You don't want a cursed woman, do you? I know you don't believe in curses, but that don't mean they aren't real."

Cate listened to all this madness with disdain. But the longer it went on, and the more she thought about it, the more she figured Aunt Flo might just be on to something. Cate looked at Gina.

Gina said, "It's worth a try. If it has no effect on the guy, then he doesn't love you and you'll be forever stuck with the curse and so you might as well marry Henry. When he kicks off in some accident it's all set up for him at the Home. Right Henry?"

"That's sick. You people are positively outrageous!"

"That's why you like to hang with us, Henry." Gina said. "Now get down and propose like a man, because I can hear them coming down the steps."

Henry pulled out the ring box, while shaking his head. He got down on one knee as he opened the tiny green velvet box. "Cate Falco—"

"Yes, yes. Give me the—whoo, it's...my God!"

"God!" Aunt Flo said, grabbing the ring. "The dead pay better than the living."

"Henry," Gina said, "I'm available."

Cate jumped up, took the ring back from Aunt Flo and pushed it on her finger. She slowly turned her hand around. She'd always thought it would be some horrible, gaudy thing that would look as if it came out of a cereal box. Instead it was beautiful. She stood staring at the mountain of blue sparkle. It had to be at least four karats—a simple round stone set in a white-gold band.

CATE FOUND RUDY and Allison in the dining room.

She took in a deep breath and said, "I've got great news."

They looked at her.

"What's that?" Rudy asked.

"I just got engaged to Henry O'Toole." She didn't say it with much force, but she had said it.

Rudy pulled away from Allison. "What? Did you say something about Henry?"

She took another deep breath and repeated, "I'm engaged to Henry O'Toole."

Rudy coughed a couple times, as if he were having some trouble breathing. Allison said, "Oh, this is so exciting. We're all getting married at the same time. It's just like in the movies. How sweet." She turned to Rudy. "Isn't it fun, sugar? Your little therapist is getting married to Harvey."

"Henry," Cate said, correcting her.

"Of course. Let's have that champagne." She took another bottle out from her bag.

"Why didn't you tell me you were engaged?" Cate asked Rudy, ignoring Allison.

"It...wasn't...it didn't happen until...it's a long story."

Can't get it out, can you, Cate thought. You're getting pulled into something you don't want. Cate put a hand on his arm, squeezed it, "I guess it's congratulations all around."

He nodded without conviction. "So, you're really engaged?"

"Yes."

"Kind of out of the blue, isn't it?"

"I guess we're under the same sky."

"Yeah, I guess we are."

Cate didn't move. Rudy didn't move. His eyes were locked on Cate's. There was something about the way he stared at her that made her believe Aunt Flo was very right about this whole thing.

He started to say something, but the doorbell rang.

"Ooh, that's your driver, sugar," Allison announced.

"Let's have that toast," Cate said. "Everybody, come on into the dining room."

Aunt Flo, Gina and Henry appeared from the kitchen. Aunt Flo in her bright-pink French tam and a matching pink scarf around her shoulders, getting a look from Allison.

Rudy popped open the bottle and they were toasting when Ted came in through the front door, stopped and surveyed the room. "What's going on?"

"We're toasting engagements, old man," Aunt Flo announced. "Have a glass of champagne. We have some celebrating to do."

Ted sat down next to her, listening in amazement to

the news. He kept shaking his head. Then he said, "I lost control over my own house, by God. First I got about a thousand reporters outside my front door, and now this."

Allison put her flute down. "Well, now that we've all had a chance to celebrate, I believe it's time to go."

"Go!" Ted bellowed.

"That's right. We have a lot to do."

With that, Allison gathered up her bag and Rudy and started to leave.

Cate followed them to the door. "This is really an amazing turn of events," she said, surreptitiously slipping a hand around Rudy's back and giving him a little rub. "It would be incredible if we could have a double wedding."

He gave her a startled look, but nothing compared to the horrified look Allison flung her way.

WHEN THEY WERE GONE, she turned to Aunt Flo and smiled. "He's fretting, big-time."

"Told you."

"What the hell's going on?" Ted yelled.

"None of your business, old man," Aunt Flo said.

"Nothin' around here seems to be my business."

"Exactly as it should be," Aunt Flo said.

"Henry," Cate said, "are you okay?"

"I'm feeling a little dizzy." He was holding his head.

"Maybe it's the champagne or something you ate. You should go home and rest. It's been a busy day for you." She gave him a gentle nudge but he didn't move.

"Everything's spinning all of a sudden," Henry said, still holding his head.

"Oh, my God," Flo said. "The curse is working already. See, Henry, you who don't believe."

"It's nothing. I'm fine. Your curse doesn't work on me. It's all voodoo nonsense."

LATER, alone in the kitchen, Aunt Flo and Cate drank coffee. Ted was asleep in his recliner in the living room and Gina was up in her room studying for a test.

"If this doesn't work, I'm doomed to wander the earth as a hexed woman." Cate cradled her head in her arms on the kitchen table. She was feeling like a complete idiot. She had put poor Henry through the ringer just to get Rudy jealous, and it was a rotten thing to do.

"Now, don't fret, doll. This is war and all's fair, like they say, in love and war."

"Yeah, but poor Henry."

"He's fine, doll. Besides, Henry's got other fish to fry, believe me. Ol' Henry gets around more than you know."

Cate felt emotionally drained by the whole evening. Rudy had been hers; she had felt it. And suddenly, without any warning, Allison shows up claiming she's pregnant.

Cate stared at her aunt for a moment, wondering if this would be a good time to ask her some questions about that kiss between her and Ted but decided against it. Enough had already happened for one day.

10

JUST AFTER ONE in the afternoon, two days after the double engagement mess, Cate was still upset that she was using poor Henry as a checkmate tactic for Rudy. She found herself trying to adjust to her low-down-dirty deed, but it wasn't happening.

She met Gina in front of Starbucks next to the Piazza DiMaggio. It was a glorious winter day, the sun bright, couples all snug in their warm coats, walking arm in arm or sitting over hot lattes in the coffee shop. It was a nice day for romance. For deception, lies and bogus engagements.

They headed for the bridal shop down the street.

"I feel miserable about this, but what else could I do?" Cate asked her sister while they shuffled through a rack of billowing wedding dresses. They had just walked into Mrs. Crocetti's bridal shop and stopped at the very first rack along the wall. Mrs. Crocetti, an older woman, walked over, made the sign of the cross, kissed the tips of her bunched fingers, looked to heaven, then stood and waited for their selections.

Mrs. Crocetti had helped Cate with her last two attempted weddings.

It seemed like all the women in the store were looking at Cate. They were probably thinking, Here we go again. The word having gotten all over the neighborhood in about twenty minutes flat. It was one of the big drawbacks of living in Little Italy.

"This is totally weird, looking for wedding dresses just to make a guy jealous. Are you sure this is okay? Like, we aren't going to be struck by lightning or anything are we?"

There were no patients scheduled at the center and The Trap hadn't called yet for Rudy's appointments—a somewhat disappointing turn of events—so Cate invited Gina to help pick out the wedding dress. Not that she would ever be wearing it down the aisle.

"No. I think we're fine. Besides, I'm just looking."

"And why are we here again?" Gina pulled out a dress covered in beads and bows. She made a face and shoved it back on the rack and moved on.

"I'm engaged. This is what engaged women do. You know how this neighborhood is." Cate nodded toward Mrs. Crocetti and the other women in the store. "I have to make it look real," she whispered, and pulled out the same beaded dress that Gina had discarded. Cate actually liked it and handed the beaded creation to Mrs. Crocetti.

"I think you're losing focus," Gina said. "How does buying a wedding dress affect Rudy? You need to be out there working to get him away from that witch."

Cate thought about it but couldn't come up with any ideas. "Like what?"

"We'll sneak in her room at night and give her a pregnancy test."

Cate laughed. "I don't think that would be happening."

"How 'bout if we follow her when they go out to eat.

When she goes to the bathroom, we get in the adjacent stalls, and hold a cup out to—"

"Stop it. You're nuts."

"We need to know the truth, here."

"Well, we need something better than sticking a cup under her butt."

They laughed so hard all the women in the store stopped what they were doing and looked at them.

Gina pulled out a simple white satin dress with virtually no back and handed it to Mrs. Crocetti. "I still don't see what good this is going to do."

"You know how gossip spreads," Cate said. "It'll get back to him that I was in here today." She took Gina's selection back from Mrs. Crocetti, thinking that it would be too shocking to show that much skin in a church, and hung it on the rack.

"I don't think this is good enough. You need to be in his face more, besides, how far are you going to take this thing with Henry? To the altar?" Gina handed Mrs. Crocetti a mini wedding dress with a sheer lace jacket and took the beads and bows back to the rack.

"If I have to. I'm a desperate woman." Cate exchanged the indecent mini for a dress with a massive satin-and-lace train.

"But what if Rudy doesn't come charging in on his white horse to save you? It's Henry, Cate. Till death do you part...now there's a scary thought," Gina said as she turned to look at Cate. She then took the long-train dress from Mrs. Crocetti and hung it up on the rack.

"It's probably what I deserve for using the poor man. Now let's try on those dresses," Cate said as she turned to Mrs. Crocetti, who stood nearby empty-handed and frowning. "We'll come back some other time."

With that, Mrs. Crocetti let out a heavy sigh, as if she had been holding her breath the entire time.

Cate took Gina's arm and they dashed from the store.

RUDY STOOD in front of a three-way mirror while Mr. Tylor, a dapper-looking man in his midfifties, measured him for a tuxedo. Rudy's bad foot rested on a black silk pillow. It didn't help. His foot, though back to a normal size, throbbed. His hip ached, his neck was tight and he was in general all around misery.

He was only here because Allison wanted to get married as soon as she could book a ballroom at the Drake Hotel. She had to fly everyone in, which, according to Allison, could be any day now, so the tux was number one on her list of his priorities.

"I was thinking of a pink tie," Rudy said to Mr. Tylor who nodded his approval.

"Pink!" Allison exclaimed, making a sour face. She stood behind the two men, with an expression of disdain.

"What's wrong with pink?" Rudy asked, thinking, I'm going to marry this girl. Married. Rudy Bellafini a husband and father!

"Don't be silly. Make it black, Mr. Taylor."

"Tylor. Black is so...so formal. Like I'm going to a funeral instead of a wedding." Mr. Tylor's eyebrows arched, but he didn't say a word, he just motioned for Rudy to hold out his arms.

"You're so sweet, sugar. Pink isn't for us. It's too common."

"Isn't that what this country is all about? The common man?"

"Only in the minds of common men, which you certainly are not."

She turned to Mr. Tylor. "Plan for a black tie, Mr. Taylor."

"Tylor. His name is Mr. Tylor."

"Taylor. Tylor. What do I care, as long as it's a black tie. Anyway, he understands me. Don't you, Taylor, honey?"

Mr. Tylor politely smiled.

Rudy hobbled away from the mirror, completely exhausted with both the conversation and his fitting. Mr. Tylor held his cloth ruler in midair.

All Rudy could think of was telling Cate the truth about the baby...if there was one. He still couldn't get Allison to a doctor, or to take another home pregnancy test. Every time he brought it up, she'd cry and then he'd apologize for tormenting her. The only battle he'd won was their having separate rooms at the hotel.

"I need to do this some other time. I'm too tired. Sorry, Allison. Mr. Tylor." Rudy walked right out of the front door of the shop. A little bell rang overhead as he left. Rudy could hear Allison's voice behind him, but because of the bell, he couldn't actually make out what she was saying, not that he cared at the moment. He needed to get away from her and think. And he needed a massage in the worst way and he didn't want Allison knowing about it.

He wondered if Cate was as good as her word and would still give him some of that magic therapy.

GINA AND CATE stood in front of Boutique a la Italia admiring a deep-red, tight-fitting, low-cut, silk gown and matching pumps. A black faux-fur coat with a matching deep-red-silk liner was displayed next to it. "Really hot," Gina said. "A woman dressed in that outfit could give a guy a reason to live."

"Or die," Cate said.

"Yeah, but what a way to go."

Cate's cell phone rang. It was her emergency service telling her that Rudy Bellafini had called in a panic.

Finally!

"It's Rudy," she told Gina and held the phone so Gina could listen in.

She immediately returned his call.

"Hello," he said after only one ring.

"You called?"

"Cate, sorry I didn't call earlier, but can you fit me into your schedule today? I'm really hurting, here."

Gina whispered. "Tell him you're busy."

Cate didn't get it, but she went along with Gina, anyway. "I don't know. It's a pretty busy day."

"I understand, but I was hoping to get a half hour of your time. That's all. Just a half hour."

Gina nodded her head.

"Well, how about this afternoon sometime?"

Gina whispered, "Now. Get him in there now."

"I can be there in fifteen minutes. Will that be all right?"

Gina twirled around. "Yes!"

"Okay," Cate said into the phone, trying to sound harried but still willing to fit him into her nonexistent tight schedule. "But I have a lot to do, so we have to stick to that half hour."

"No problem. I'll meet you at the center."

She hung up. "He's back!"

"Do you want me to come with you?" Gina asked.

Cate said, "No. I can handle him now. I think I know what I have to do."

A bus drove by spewing its acrid diesel fumes into the air. It made Cate sneeze.

"Be careful. No kissing unless it's absolutely necessary, Cate. Promise," Gina insisted.

Cate held up her hand. "I promise not to kiss Rudy Bellafini. I'm fine. Really. I'm in complete control over the situation." Then she sneezed three times in a row. Cate figured it had something to do with her curse, and little to do with the bus.

She was getting used to lying to Rudy. To Henry. To just about everyone. It was easy once she put her mind to it. Once she grabbed hold of it and decided that hell was a lot better than celibacy.

RUDY LAY ON HIS STOMACH with his arms tucked along his sides and his long muscular legs stretched down to the tip of the table. He barely fit. He was naked except for his briefs and a towel placed over his backside.

It was a slow day at the Wellness Center. Mr. Fried, a plumber with lower-back problems walked on a treadmill while Jennie Santelli, a florist, learned some stretches from Mava Clark, another therapist at the center.

Cate and Rudy were in a private room with the door open.

Cate spilled a few drops of the musky massage oil onto her hands and started with his neck. She wanted to get him completely relaxed and comfortable before she started asking him questions. "Tell me if this hurts," she instructed.

As soon as she applied pressure, he jerked.

"Sorry." Getting him relaxed was going to take some doing. Instead of him getting better, he seemed to have remained the same or gotten worse. Not exactly a sign of prenuptial bliss, she thought.

"No problem. I guess I really needed this. Missing a couple days was a pretty bad idea, huh?"

"You should come in every day this week." She eased up on the pressure and could feel him releasing some of his tension.

"Sure, as long as you can fit me in."

Rudy was still playing the Mr. Nice Guy routine, all sympathetic to Cate's time and work schedule. It seemed that every time she gave him a massage, the good Rudy came out and she would forget the purpose of her mission.

"Anytime...I mean, we'll work something out."

His body started to warm under her hands. She concentrated on his shoulders and neck while she thought of how to ask him about Allison.

"So, like, are you really going through with it?" Rudy asked.

"Through with what?" She knew exactly what he was talking about, and loved that he actually seemed jealous. She wanted him to think she was so comfortable with her wedding that it was the furthest thing from her mind.

"Marrying Henry?"

"As sure as you're marrying Allison."

"Yeah."

She said, "You have good genes, Rudy, you should have kids."

"What?"

"Kids. You should have a bunch. A whole Olympic team full."

"What are you talking about?"

"You're at that age. You're getting married to a beautiful woman. Don't you want children?"

"Yes, of course I want children. But I wasn't planning...is there some other subject we can talk about?"

"Sure. Which would you prefer, a girl or boy for your first child?"

He was squirming now. Keeping his little secret. "Rudy, I have to say," she put some pressure on his back "this Allison thing came as a big shock. Not that I haven't been shocked by you before."

"Sorry about that. I was going to tell you. It's not like you think."

"Oh! What am I supposed to think?" He groaned when she put a little too much pressure on his lower back. "Is there something you want to tell me?"

He sighed. "Allison's pregnant."

There it was, out in the open.

"Are you sure?"

"What do you mean?"

"Did you see the test results?"

"No. But I can't see her lying about something this big. Not when I'd find out soon enough."

"Like after you're married? All she'd have to do is fake losing it."

He turned his shoulders and pushed up and looked at her. He started to say something, then didn't. He turned and fell back on the table.

After a time he said, "Do you love Henry?"

"There are many reasons to get married. He's a very nice man and he loves me."

"That's not enough. If you don't love him—"

"Do you love Allison? Or are you marrying her because she's pregnant?"

"That's different."

"Is it?"

"Isn't he kind of...well, old? I mean, he was old when we were kids. He must be—"

"Smart. At least Henry's smart. Nobody plays him for a fool." She slid her thumbs along the back of his neck and dug into his shoulders, increasing the pressure.

"What's that supposed to mean?"

"It means what I said, at least the man is smart. That's more than I can say for some other people."

"Like me?"

"If the shoe fits."

She put all her strength into his massage. He started squirming around on the table like a mackerel caught on the end of a hook.

"Why did she push you off that lift? What were you arguing about?"

"It was an accident. She had nothing to do with my fall."

"Well, good, because if you fall off the El there won't be anybody around to pick up the pieces."

"Cate, does it have to hurt so much? I'm dying here."

He pushed himself up from the table. She took a step back and said, "Yeah, well, aren't we all."

They stared at each other for a moment.

"Yoo-hoo! Anybody here?" Allison called from the lobby. Her timing perfect.

"You can leave or work on the machines for a while. Either one is fine with me," Cate said.

He started to say something, but Allison blew in, wearing a fake smile that matched her fake personality. "I thought I'd find you here with your little therapist."

Cate smiled, but she wanted to smack the woman right across her bright-pink chops, which probably wouldn't do enough damage so she did the next best thing. "I'm having an engagement party next Friday night, and you're both invited. It's at the top of the Italian American Sports Hall of Fame at seven-thirty. It's going to be the biggest party Taylor Street has ever seen. Really. You have to come."

Rudy said, "I think we have other plans that night."

"Oh, don't be silly, sugar. We can't miss Cat's little engagement party."

"Cate. Her name is Cate," Rudy barked.

"Oh, don't be silly, sugar," Cate said, mimicking Allison. "Cat's a fine name. A smart name. Don't you agree?"

Rudy grunted, wrapped the towel around his waist, slipped off the table and left the room. "I'll be right out."

Allison looked uncomfortable being left alone in the room with her.

Cate said, "So, Rudy tells me you're pregnant."

Allison gave her an empty look, like she didn't know what she was talking about. Then caught herself. "Yes, isn't it wonderful? I've always wanted children. I can't think of a man on earth I'd rather have for the father of my children than Rudy."

"How many months are you?"

"Um, well, four. I think. I really haven't been keeping track."

"A doctor can tell you. I have a wonderful gynecologist. Can I make an appointment for you? It's important to know how far along the pregnancy is."

"I'm sure it is. I'll be going to my doctor in L.A. But thanks."

"No problem."

You, my dear, are about as pregnant as Aunt Flo's dead cat, Cate thought. You won't get away with this.

CATE AND HENRY STOOD together in the back of one of his viewing parlors at the funeral home. An empty, open casket sat up front, and the Crying Lady knelt beside it on a kneeler.

"What's she doing?" Cate whispered.

"Practicing."

The Crying Lady let out a long sorrowful mourn. Cate had come to the home to talk to Henry. Seeing the Crying Lady actually practicing reminded Cate of her own future if she didn't break the curse.

"Henry, we need to have an engagement party."

"Certainly, but we don't—"

"Next Friday."

Henry sat down on a folding chair. "Is that necessary? Is this plan of yours going to work? What if it doesn't? I'm not liking this much. Everybody is congratulating me everywhere I go. I'm lying to all of them. And when they find out, I'll be a laughingstock."

Cate felt bad for him. She never meant this to happen. On the other hand, it would put an end to his hopeless quest for her hand and that would free him in a way. So she began to see this as good for Henry. Just what he needed.

The Crying Lady began sobbing.

"You don't have to worry about a thing, Henry. I'll take care of everything. All you have to do is show up."

"But shouldn't we plan this together?" He was almost yelling. The Crying Lady had taken off with her wailing and the whole room seemed to echo her voice.

"You're too busy to worry about minor details."

"Well, I did get a call from Carmen Petrassi today. One of his buddies had an accident."

Carmen's name gave her pause, but she let it go. "See what I mean?" Cate gave him the information but he couldn't quite hear her.

"Excuse me, dear," he told Cate, and turned to the Crying Lady. "Stella. Stella. Hold it down."

She immediately stopped and dried her eyes on a frilly hankie.

"All right. Now go on."

Cate repeated herself, and when she finished Henry stood up.

"You know, we haven't even kissed yet, and we're having an engagement party," Henry said. "It might not be the real thing, but I deserve at least a fake kiss." He puckered his lips and leaned in for a big one.

Cate leaned back and said, "Henry. I'm surprised at you. We can't kiss in a viewing room. It's bad luck."

"We can go outside."

"That would be even worse luck."

Then as if on cue, Crying Lady Stella let out a glass-shattering wail.

"AN ENGAGEMENT PARTY!" Gina repeated for about the tenth time. "What were you thinking?"

Cate sat between Gina and Aunt Flo inside a local wine bar while a wicked snowstorm raged. Francesca's was beautifully furnished in shades of gold, deep greens and rich burgundy. A rather large painting of the backside of a nude woman hung on one wall, while ornate masks of laughing jesters adorned the others. Normally, it was the place Cate liked to come for friendly conversation and a relaxed atmosphere, but not tonight. Tonight she felt as if all the jesters were sneering and the nude was laughing behind that svelte backside of hers.

"She was thinking Rudy needs a little more coaxing, and what better way than an engagement party," Aunt Flo said. "Right, doll?" Cate didn't answer. "And we're gonna make it the best darn engagement party this neighborhood has ever seen."

"Where did you say this thing was going to take place?"

"The top of the Italian American Sports Hall of Fame."

Gina sat back on the velvet sofa. "Of course. The Falco girls have all their engagement parties up there."

"Okay. We can handle this," Aunt Flo said.

"But there's so much to do. How are we ever going to get it all done? It's less than a week away. I must have been nuts or something. Sometimes things come out of my mouth, but there's somebody else saying the words." Cate picked up her glass and took a couple sips of the fruity wine.

"Doll, it's going to be fabulous! All you gotta worry about is looking like a queen."

"I can help with that," Gina said.

"But what about the decorations and the food and the drinks and all the people?" Cate sat back, exhausted just thinking about it. The lights flickered.

"I got a few days off coming to me. I'll take 'em and take care of everything. You know how I love this kind of stuff. I'll get my bunco group to help. You'll see. It'll be wonderful. Better than any of your other engagement parties."

"I never had any other engagement parties."

"Well, this will be your best one then," Aunt Flo said.

That's when the lights went out.

IT TOOK ALMOST EIGHT HOURS for the electricity to come back on, and during those eight hours Cate wondered if the blackout wasn't somehow her fault for all the lying and manipulating she was doing. Maybe God was trying to warn her of her evil ways.

Or it was just a blackout.

The next day, Gina, Aunt Flo and Cate went to work on the party, inviting everyone they could think of, contacting the hall with the details, ordering the food, the wine and the music.

By two o'clock on the following Friday afternoon, there was nothing left for Cate to do but get ready. She needed to look her best.

At two-thirty Cate sat in a green chair at The Hair's End and listened to Rose Marie, a short, big-boned woman, describe the latest trends in hairstyles. "I've been waitin' to get my hands on your hair for a long time." She ran her fingers through Cate's hair. "What kinda look you want? Big hair is comin' back this year, but I don't know if it's right for you."

She took a step back from the chair, tapped her index finger on her chin and stared at Cate's unruly locks. "Maybe somethin' more dramatic. I can fix you up with anything and any color. Red. Black. Brown. Pink or purple. Whatever you want, Rose Marie can do it."

"Just cover up any gray hairs," Cate told her.

"You want to pay sixty bucks for me to take the gray out? You can do that at home for ten. Let me give you a new look. It's time. Besides, don't you want to look good for that party of yours tonight?"

Cate thought it over and decided that she not only wanted to look good for her party, but she wanted to look spectacular, and Rose Marie was just the girl who could do spectacular.

"Okay," Cate said. "Give me the works."

"Now you're talkin'." Rose Marie beamed.

First she dyed Cate's hair a soft brown, and streaked it with fiery auburn highlights. Then she razor-cut it in shorter layers, to give it that wind-blown, totally-now look.

She tweezed Cate's eyebrows, gave her a facial and even bleached the hair on her upper lip.

Then came a manicure and a pedicure. By the time Cate stepped out of the chair she felt like a new woman. Rose Marie's makeover had been a complete success.

"You look like a million bucks," she said as Cate walked out of the shop. "Now all you need are the clothes to go with that million bucks."

Cate knew just the dress she wanted to buy.

11

RUDY WALKED INTO Allison's bathroom while she was putting on makeup for Cate's engagement party. She said, "How do I look?"

He laid a bag from the drugstore on the counter. "You look fine."

"What's that?"

"It's a home pregnancy test kit."

She whirled around. "If you think I'm lying—"

"Don't start the tear routine. It won't work. I have a right to know the truth."

"You don't believe me?"

"I don't know what to believe. That's why we have science."

"I'm not taking a test. Besides, I'm dressed for the party. We'll talk about this later."

"No."

She turned to him now. She had that look he knew so well. The same look when they were arguing on the chairlift. He took a half step back.

"I'm the woman you are going to marry. I'm the woman who's going to have your children. We have to start with trust."

"No, we have to start with a pregnancy test."

She grabbed the bag and threw it at him. Despite any leftover pain from his earlier injuries Rudy was still quick and ducked just in time. The bag landed on the floor. He picked it up.

"If you don't take the test, I'm walking out. I'll assume you aren't pregnant. I won't come back."

"You bastard!"

"You just have to pee on a stick. It's not that big a deal. Just do it and we'll have this resolved once and for all."

"It's her, isn't it. That little bitch with the magic touch."

"It's about whether you're pregnant. That's what it's about."

"You're sleeping with her, aren't you? You want to be honest, let's start with you."

"No, I'm not sleeping with her."

"You're a liar."

He knew where this was headed. She wanted the battle to turn to him defending his actions. Not this time. This time she was the one who had to prove her honesty. He held up the test. "You either take this test or we can just say goodbye right now."

He tossed the bag on the vanity.

She glared at him, ignoring the bag. That told him all he needed to know. He turned and headed for the door.

Allison came after him. "Don't you walk out on me, damn you. You come back here!"

He opened the door and looked back at her. "Frankly, my dear, I never did give a damn."

She grabbed the nearest object, a small table lamp, and threw it in his direction. It reached the end of the cord length and snapped back and almost hit her in the head.

He walked out, shut the door and moved toward the elevator. He felt a sense of accomplishment. More than that, a sense that he'd finally made a critical decision in his life about women. Too many was a really bad thing. One was handful enough. And the one he wanted was about to marry an undertaker.

How mixed-up could things get?

IT WAS ONE OF THOSE perfectly clear and crisp Chicago nights that Cate loved. She stood on the sidewalk outside the Italian American Sports Hall of Fame, taking it all in, then made her way up to the banquet room of the Rooftop Café. She lingered again in the doorway. The view was dazzling. The Hancock Building and the Sears Tower glistened off in the distance, and the city lights danced across the moonless sky. The café itself was awash with Italian flair.

Aunt Flo and the ladies of the Saint Mary's bunco club had outdone themselves. Gold mesh surrounded candy-covered almonds in miniature bags next to gold-trimmed plates on every table, and there were plenty of tables, at least thirty. Each table sat six and was filled with family, friends and a few people Cate didn't recognize.

There was a gold tissue paper, accordion wedding bell in the center of each of the tables, and cousin Charlie and his band, Hot Diggity, played an old Perry Como tune, "Don't Let The Stars Get In Your Eyes."

On the way up to the café, Cate had passed Rudy's picture and dedication. He was in several poses, mugging for the camera, wearing his three gold medals. Because he was local, the Hall of Fame had a complete wall dedicated to him. Cate stopped in front of it for a moment, remembering how he had looked, up on that podium, receiving medal number three. It was just about the same time cute Paul had gotten stuck in a revolving door.

As she stood in the entrance to the café, Henry walked over to her, carrying a white jasmine corsage. "Can I take your coat?" he asked.

"Yes," she said, and slipped it off.

Henry's startled eyes just about shot out of his head. "You. You. What I mean is—" He coughed.

"Get it under control, Henry," she told him.

He tugged on his shirt collar. "You look lovely tonight, Cate."

"Thanks, Henry. Is that for me?" She pointed to the corsage.

"Yes. Yes they are," he said and handed her the box. "Are you going to be warm enough? I mean, there's not much to that dress. I mean—" He took a deep breath and let it out. "I wouldn't want you to catch cold."

She pinned the tiny jasmine corsage above her left breast and said, "This is all I'll need. Thanks, Henry."

He blushed and tried to smile.

Cate took his arm, and they walked into the room, together.

TED BLAMED IT on the fact that Henry had gotten new dentures and wasn't used to the fit, and that the chocolate-covered canolli were especially hard. It could have happened to anybody.

Maybe.

Aunt Flo tried to blame it on old age, that when you

reach a certain decade you're no longer aware of the food in your mouth and you forget what you're eating.

A nice try.

Gina said that Henry tried to talk with his mouth full.

Could be.

The Crying Lady didn't say a word. She just kept crying.

Always an option in times of crisis.

But Cate blamed it on the curse.

The truth was Henry had in fact gotten new dentures, and the chocolate-covered canolli was actually as hard as a rock. True, he ate it too fast, but when he started choking at his own engagement party, during Ted's toast for "a long and happy life together" everyone thought Henry was overcome with joy, not overcome with a stuck canolli.

So when Vinney and his crew arrived, the guests cleared out to give them room. Cousin Charlie and his band stopped playing while everybody waited out on the front sidewalk for word on Henry's fate.

As Henry started to come around, Cate didn't even wait for him to break off the engagement. She simply slipped his ring off her finger, tucked it safely into Henry's jacket pocket and watched along with the neighborhood as the paramedics carted him off to the hospital, happy to be alive.

She had wanted to go with him, to make sure he would be all right, but Vinney told her it might be better if she wasn't there when he woke up. "Seeing you could send him over the edge, if you know what I mean."

"There goes another one," Ted said to Aunt Flo as

they stood in front of the glass doors of the Italian American Hall of Fame and watched as the lights from the ambulance faded into the night.

"At least he's breathing," Aunt Flo said. She stood next to Ted, her arm tucked into his, reminding Cate that she still hadn't told Gina about that kiss, but now most definitely was not the time. Cate was so shook up she could hardly think, let alone divulge some bizarre kiss episode involving their dad.

"I was hoping it wouldn't get him because it wasn't a real engagement. So much for that theory. This is one strong curse." Aunt Flo shook her head in amazement.

Cate watched from inside the lobby as the ambulance drove off with Henry. She couldn't speak. She couldn't move. All she could think of was that stinking, no good, rotten curse and Rudy Bellafini, who hadn't even bothered to show up.

RUDY SAT in the Starbucks next to Piazza DiMaggio, perusing the morning edition of the *Chicago Sun Times* for the latest gossip on his affairs. After his argument with Allison last night, he thought for sure she would have contacted the media with the details, but the paper was clean.

As he contented himself on a second grande Mocha Cappuccino with a triple shot of espresso, he overheard someone mention Cate's name. He couldn't help but listen in on the conversation from the table directly across from him.

"I suppose you heard about Henry O'Toole, then," a girl with bright red hair said.

"Oh, yeah. They had to cart the poor bastard away in

an ambulance," the guy said looking up from his laptop.

"You gotta wonder why anybody would even date Cate Falco. The girl is like the plague."

"Is he dead?" the guy asked.

"I wouldn't be surprised."

Rudy's coffee suddenly soured in his stomach. "Excuse me," Rudy said. "I don't want to seem rude, but I couldn't help but overhear your conversation. I'm a friend of Henry's. Do you know where they took him?"

The young couple gave Rudy the details, and he took off for the Illinois Medical Center just a few blocks away.

"HENRY O'TOOLE'S ROOM, please," Cate said into the phone the next morning as soon as she opened her eyes and was able to dial. Sunshine poured in through the curtainless living room windows causing her headache to intensify. She had fallen asleep in the recliner, and now she couldn't move her neck.

"Are you a family member?" the operator asked.

Cate didn't like the question. What difference did it make if she were a family member or not? "Yes. I'm his fiancée, or was, but it doesn't matter now."

"You're right. It doesn't matter. I'll connect you to the nurse's station on his floor. Please wait."

Cate listened to the silence on the other end of the phone when a shot of fear swept through her.

"Oh, God!" she said out loud and hung up.

Twenty minutes later, after brushing her teeth, washing her face, and downing three aspirin, Cate knelt inside a confessional at Saint Mary's Church. She still wore the blood-red dress from the night before so she kept her coat buttoned up tight.

"Bless me, Father, for I have sinned." She touched her forehead and shoulders, blessing herself.

"What seems to be troubling you, Cate, that I had to hear your confession on this lovely morning?" Father Joe asked.

"Thank you, but I can't go on unless I know what to do."

"I'm listening."

"My life's a mess, Father. I've lied. I've cheated and I've killed another one."

"Another one, what?"

"Another fiancé. Does it count if I didn't do it on purpose? I mean, I thought because he wasn't a real fiancé or boyfriend he would be safe."

"Real?"

"Never mind about that."

Cate let out a heavy sigh. "I've killed Henry O'Toole. Just tell me one thing, am I too old to join a convent?"

"What makes you think you've killed Henry?"

"I called the hospital this morning and, well, I couldn't talk to him."

"Of course you couldn't."

"See what I mean? I've killed him."

"Cate, Henry left on a morning flight for Florida."

"What?"

"He and Stella Barcio are on their way to get married, and—"

"Crying Lady Stella and Henry are getting married?"

"Yes. They were in a hurry. Henry came to his senses, he said, and decided he'd really loved Stella all along. I blessed them on my rounds this morning at the hospital. Rudy Bellafini was there. Wonderful fellow, that Rudy. He gave them two first-class tickets to Miami as a wedding present. What a generous man. It was good to see him again. By the way, I've been meaning to call you, I've got this pain—"

But Cate was out the door.

SHE HAD TO TRACK DOWN Rudy Bellafini and get him back, marry him and end this catastrophe. There was no way Allison was telling him the truth, and she was going to make him find out.

When he didn't answer his cell phone and had no real friends in the neighborhood, tracking him down was no small task for Cate, but she did it. Somehow she knew Aunt Flo would know where he was hiding. Cate gave her a call and, sure enough, Aunt Flo knew exactly where Rudy Bellafini, the miserable little worm, was hiding.

"Oh, doll," she said. "I'm over at Rudy's restaurant tasting pasta sauces. It's so much fun! You should come."

Cate hung up, grabbed a cab and arrived at his rotten restaurant on Wells Street in less than the time it took for Aunt Flo to figure out that Cate wasn't on the phone anymore.

Cate burst through the front door on a mission. The restaurant hadn't opened yet, so the place was virtually empty except for Aunt Flo, Rudy and a group of men and women dressed in white chef jackets. The bevy of chefs stood around Rudy's table.

"How dare you?" Cate roared.

"Are you talking to me?" Rudy asked, pointing back at himself.

"You know I am. How dare you?"

"How dare I what?"

"Ruin my life. How dare you send my fiancé off to Florida!"

He stood up...slowly. She could tell that his hip was giving him some pain.

"You don't love Henry. The Crying Lady, now that's the girl for Henry. You should have seen the look on her face when Henry proposed. His ring looks even better on her hand than it did yours. It suits her. I think she actually cracked a smile."

Cate wanted to crack something, all right, but it wasn't a smile.

Aunt Flo said, "Come and sit down, doll. Rudy's got some good pasta sauces here. You should taste 'em."

"I don't want any sauces."

"Why not? I had my chefs cook them up because of that great sauce of yours. None finer," Rudy told her. He wiped his mouth on a white linen napkin, then neatly placed it on the table beside his plate.

"You're avoiding the issue." Her hands went up to her hips. She was steaming mad now.

"And the issue being?"

"Us. You and me. I can't take it anymore. I want a normal life, with a normal husband. You have to marry me. I know Allison is lying. You have to confront her. You have to make her take a test."

"Doll, I don't think this is the right way—"

"You stay out of this," Cate said, then felt badly for having been so sharp with her aunt, but these were drastic times.

"Marry you! Where'd you get this bright idea?"

"You gave it to me ten years ago."

He stared at her. She stared back, determined to get him this time.

"You're not serious." He turned to Aunt Flo. "She's not serious, is she?"

"Yeah, hon, I think she is," Aunt Flo said.

"You bet I'm serious. If you don't marry me, I'll...I'll stop all treatment. You'll have to go somewhere else. I won't ever touch you again. Ever. Never. And...I'll call the *Trib.* and *People* and the *L.A. Times,* and anybody else I can think of and tell them what a lying, cheating jilter you really are." It all sounded pretty lame, but it was the best she could do.

Rudy gave her a gotcha smile. "So, you want me to give up my impending marriage. My ready-to-go family."

"Why not? Because she's pregnant? That's bull. You don't love her."

"How do you know that?"

"I'm a woman, and women know. *Do* you love her?"

Rudy looked her straight in the eye. "No. I don't love her."

Cate moved forward, and even though her hair wasn't great, and she wore no makeup, she knew the dress still looked fantastic. She slipped off her coat.

"Oh, doll," Aunt Flo said.

Rudy did a once-over. Then a twice-over as she took another step in his direction.

He took a step backward toward the wall and hesitated. "There's a lot to love about Allison, but—"

Cate walked straight for him, put her arms around

his neck, pushed him up against the wall and kissed him.

This time Cate kissed him with everything that was in her. She let herself go. Let herself feel all the passion. Her tongue played with his. Her lips burned with desire. If the earth opened and swallowed them up, she wouldn't even notice the fall.

Rudy returned her kiss with the same intensity. With the same fire. If they had been alone, they would've been ripping their clothes off, but they weren't alone. Aunt Flo was there. The ten chefs were there and... Allison.

The plate of sauce hitting the wall right next to their heads brought them out of their kiss trance.

"Of all the—" Allison said as the thick, rich, red sauce slid down the wall. Both Cate and Rudy were covered with splats of pasta sauce. The heavy plate had missed Rudy's head by a millimeter before it exploded on the wall. Cate had actually felt it whiz by the tip of her left ear.

Rudy stepped away from Cate and made an attempt to stop Allison, but as soon as he took his first step, he slipped on the sauce and hit the floor faster than you could say, *"Arrivederci."*

"You won't get away with this, Rudy," Allison yelled. "Not this time! I knew you were having an affair with her! And I'm glad I'm not really pregnant. I wouldn't want your damn kid. It'd be just like you, a real jerk." Allison turned and stomped out of the restaurant in a flurry of self-righteous bravado. Her high-heeled boots clicked a fond farewell on the orange tile as she marched out the front door.

Cate knelt down to check on Rudy, and when she

did, her breasts nearly popped out of her dress. He had no choice but to stare right at them.

"So, I guess I was right."

"Apparently women know these things."

"Then we're getting married. Right?" Cate asked.

"Right," Rudy mumbled.

"How does next Saturday sound?"

"Anything you want, Cate Falco. I'll marry you in a week, a day or right now, if that's what you want." He rested his head in her lap, and closed his eyes.

"Boy, it's hot in here," Aunt Flo said, fanning herself with her white napkin.

Cate sat back on her heels and wiped the dripping sauce off her own cheek and tasted it, swirling it around in her mouth like a fine wine. "Close," she said. "But a little too much basil, don't you think?"

"Whatever you say, doll," her aunt said, still fanning herself. "Whatever you say."

12

THE WEEK HAD FLOWN BY since Rudy had said yes to Cate's proposal, and Rudy was adjusting to the idea much better than he'd anticipated. But everyone else around him seemed to be having some kind of problem. He couldn't quite figure out what that was. Some stupid curse thing.

It started that day at the hospital when Henry kept harping on some crazy curse that Cate was under. And unless Rudy did something about it, every man that Cate touched would self-destruct. Rudy even heard the same thing from a couple of the nurses, and one of the doctors told him a story about one of Cate's boyfriends getting caught in a revolving door.

Just before Henry and Stella had left the hospital, Henry had convinced Rudy that he was the only man alive immune to her curse, and it was about time he stepped up to the plate and resolved this thing.

"I'll take two cards," he told Vinney as they sat around an old wooden table in cousin Charlie's basement. The men, Vinney, Charlie and two guys from their old high school, Paulie and Marko, had been playing for about two hours. The basement reeked of a combination of wine and cigar smoke, just the way Rudy remembered it.

The whole place was never quite finished: the floor was black cement, the walls were gray cement and the ceiling was a mixture of black-oak beams and plaster. The room was kept warm by an old coal stove, which accounted for everything being soot-black. To add to the ambiance, oak barrels filled with some of the best homemade red wine around lined each wall and filled up every inch of unused floor space.

The cold-storage room in the back held Charlie's wife's canning. Rudy couldn't even begin to name all that was put up back there, but he did remember the jars of hot peppers, tomato sauce, pickled eggplant, and the drying pepperoni hanging from the ceiling. All of which, in one form or another, he had consumed during the card game. What he liked most was the red wine, and after four glasses, it just got better and better.

Vinney did the dealing, and Rudy, for now, did the betting.

"I'll see your quarter and raise you a dime," Rudy said to Charlie, who was busy eyeing the pot worth at least $1.50.

"That's too strong for me. I'm out," he said, and threw his cards into the center.

"Aha! Got ya again," Rudy gleefully said as he raked in the change to his side of the table. Of course, raking the change in required a little more effort, now that his arm was in a sling from his fall in the restaurant.

Vinney gathered all the cards and shuffled. "That arm of yours looks almost healed."

"Yeah," Rudy said as he twisted his wrist. It didn't really hurt anymore, a little stiff, but no actual pain. Matter of fact, his whole body was feeling almost normal these days. Cate had been giving him daily massages, which were great, but no matter how passionate the massages had gotten, he still wasn't able to get her into bed. The whole thing was driving him crazy.

"I'll tell ya, man, be extra cautious with everything you do in the next twenty-four hours," Vinney told him. "I don't want no phone calls at the station to clean up Rudy Bellafini off the street or nothing."

Paulie and Marko nodded their heads in agreement. "Yeah, be careful, man," Marko said in a gruff voice. Marko was short and stout. Paulie was tall and thin. Paulie married Maggie, Marko's little sister, and Marko married Pauline, Paulie's older sister. Rudy guessed the guys didn't like to stray too far from their nest.

"Nothing's going to happen *before* the wedding," Charlie said.

Charlie was a mountain of a man, with jet-black hair and dark brown eyes, who liked to sing old Perry Como tunes whenever he had the chance. According to Cate, Charlie would be crooning those tunes at their wedding.

Rudy looked over at Charlie, thinking that was a curious statement. "What does that mean?" Rudy asked. He took a sip of wine. It was as smooth as any thirty-dollar bottle of Chianti.

"I'm not the one to be telling you about that kind of stuff. That's private. That's between you and Cate." He chomped on his unlit cigar. His wife didn't want him to smoke, so he just chewed on the thing and pretended, for the most part. But every now and then he'd light it up, take a puff or two and put it out again.

Charlie blushed.

Vinney dealt the cards. "That's not what he means,

Charlie. I think he wants you to tell him if you know anything else about Cate's curse."

"You shouldn't say it like that, Vinney. People are gonna get the wrong idea about my cousin." He nodded his head toward Paulie and Marko.

Rudy took a drag on his cigar, blew it out and said, "Tell you what, guys, at this point, feeling the way I do—" he moved his shoulders around, twisted his wrist and took the sling completely off "—I don't care about anything but this card game. And I'm feeling lucky, so look out, cause the only curse at this table is the one I'm putting on you rummies."

AUNT FLO, Cate and Gina sat together at Rosebuds restaurant on Taylor Street getting ready to order dinner when Cate noticed that Aunt Flo was busy wiping her eyes while trying to hide behind her menu.

"Aunt Flo, what's wrong?" Cate asked.

"Nothing. Nothing. Don't worry about me. This is your night," she said, and blew her nose on a tissue. "You shouldn't have to worry about your old-maid aunt the night before you break your curse. I mean, it don't matter that I'll never get the chance to do what you're doing, and I gotta live under this damn thing till the day I die."

Gina rolled her eyes at Cate and said, "Aunt Flo, you don't know for sure that your curse is the same as Cate's. You've never dated anybody else since Pinky. How do you know you're really cursed?"

Aunt Flo sat back in her seat. "A cursed woman knows these things. How did I know that woman wasn't pregnant?"

Cate said, without even thinking, "Did something happen between you and my dad?"

Gina said, "What does Dad have to do with this?"

Aunt Flo slapped the table. Everything on it rattled. Her eyes seemed to instantly dry up and she developed a threatening scowl on her face. A few of the people at the surrounding tables looked over. "Who's been spreading rumors? Tell me and I'll go right over, right now and straighten this person out."

She stood up.

"Aunt Flo, sit down. People are looking," Gina said.

"Their noses should fall off." She turned and made a face at the older couple sitting next to her, and they immediately went back to their dinners.

"So that's what it looks like," Cate said.

"That's what *what* looks like?" Aunt Flo asked.

"The evil eye."

Aunt Flo sat down. "What? You never seen it before?"

"Not up close like that."

"Well, that wasn't it."

"If it wasn't, then why are those two leaving?" Cate watched as the older couple left the restaurant in a hurry.

"They got someplace else to go." Aunt Flo dunked a piece of bread in the small plate of olive oil in the middle of the table. "Your father and me had a fight and I don't want to see him ever again."

Gina pleaded. "Okay, will somebody *please* tell me what's going on?"

They ignored her question. Cate said, "But you'll see him at my wedding tomorrow."

"That's the last time."

"You come over for dinner almost every night."

"I won't look at him."

"Guys. Guys. What's all this about?" Gina held her hands out across the table to get their attention.

Aunt Flo looked over at her. "Your father and me have been spending time together. No official dates. He's too old, if something should happen because of the curse. I mean, he could break a hip. So, I show up at places and if he's there, then we have a nice time together. If he's not, I go home."

"You're dating my dad?" Gina said.

"We don't date!" Aunt Flo slammed the table again, but this time no one looked over.

Gina grabbed a wineglass before it tumbled. "I got it. But if you meet and have a nice time together, why are you crying?"

"Because for two nights now, I showed up at different places and your father wasn't there."

"Did he know where to go?" Cate asked.

"Of course not. Then it would be a date."

Gina sat back in her chair. "And you're mad because he couldn't find you?"

"There are only so many places I can be. He should know these things."

Cate said, "Isn't that my dad standing by the bar?"

Aunt Flo leaned over and took a look. "So, he finally figured it out. Excuse me, girls. I gotta go talk to your father and get this thing straightened out."

When she left the table, Gina said, "Okay, now that I'm in total shock, fess up. What's going on?"

Cate spent the next fifteen minutes filling Gina in on the total Aunt Flo and Dad sighting. When she finished her story, Gina said, "God, they could get married or something."

"Mamma Flo."

They stared at each other, wide-eyed. "Oh, my God!" they said in unison.

"Don't worry about a thing, girls," Aunt Flo said, returning to the table. "Your father and me got it all worked out."

Gina and Cate tried to regain their composure, but Cate was having trouble picturing Aunt Flo as her stepmom.

"Get the lemon chicken, doll," Aunt Flo told Cate. "The lemon will keep your breath sweet for the wedding. There's nothing worse than a bride with stinking breath."

Cate could only nod.

Aunt Flo continued. "This is a happy occasion. We're here to talk about your beautiful wedding tomorrow." She picked up her knife and wiped it off with her napkin. "So, when are you gonna run out on the dirty rat?"

I'M DRUNK," Rudy said, as he stood at Cate's front door.

"What are you doing here? It's late," she said.

"I want to spend the night." He leaned in, and she got a good whiff. His clothes reeked of stale wine and cigar smoke.

She pushed him back. "You can't stay here. Go home."

"But I'm lost. I don't know where I live anymore, where I belong. Take me upstairs to your bed. I like your bed. It's pink, just like you."

"No. You're going to wake up the whole neighborhood. Now go home." She tried to push him away from her front porch, but he wouldn't budge.

He took hold of her hand. "Come on. Let's make love. We used to do that all the time when we were engaged the first time. Why can't we do it now?"

"Because we should wait until after our vows."

"Who says?"

"I do."

"I do, too."

"You do what?"

"Whatever you want me to do. I do."

"Go home. You're not making any sense."

"But none of this makes sense. I think we're dumb. That's what we are. Dumb. I think we should at least kiss once in a while. Just so people won't get the wrong idea. Come on and kiss me the way you did in my restaurant." He lunged for her, mouth puckered, eyes shut. He looked like some kind of weird fish.

She pushed him away, and this time he nearly fell over. She closed the front door and went inside. He stood there yelling her name. "Cate. Cate Falco. Come out, come out wherever you are."

She slipped on her coat, scarf and hat thinking there was no getting rid of him when he was in this state. She opened the door. He stood leaning up against the wall, smiling at nothing in particular. Just smiling. She thought he looked awfully cute when he smiled like that, as if he didn't have a care in the world. As if he were a little boy waiting for his friend to come out and play. "Come on. I'll walk you home." She found herself grinning back at him.

Her big fear was that he still might bolt before she

got the chance to dump him and break the curse. What a disaster that would be. So she had to play this right. And be with him all the time. All week she'd had somebody watching him. She never gave him the chance to start thinking. She had him and she was holding on tight until she finished this. She felt bad about it at times. But it was necessary. Part of her, of course, never wanted to let him go.

"Take in some slow, deep breaths. It's good for you," she told him as they walked down the sidewalk toward his house. She tucked her arm through his to steady him.

He drew in a couple deep breaths, then coughed. It was a cold, crisp night, and the mist from his breath billowed up on his face making him look almost angelic, but she knew better. Rudy Bellafini was no angel.

"How'd you get like this?" she asked.

"Years of neglect."

"I don't mean in general. I mean how did you get like this tonight?"

"Oh. Yes. Tonight. I had a hell of a good time. Won $3.75 at last count. Or was it $2.65? I can't remember."

"Then, you were gambling?"

"I think that's what it was. Yes."

"At Charlie's?"

"How'd you know that? Not only are you beautiful, but you're perceptive as well."

"My own cousin's wrecking my fiancé."

"But I'm not wrecked. Three weeks ago I was wrecked. But not now. Not since your magic touch. Do I look wrecked?"

He turned and stood in front of her, held his arms out and swayed as he tried to keep his balance. She had to smile in spite of herself. He looked too adorable with those cute big brown eyes and that luscious brown hair all curly around his face.

"You're drunk," she said. "That's what you are, and I bet it's from Charlie's homemade wine."

"You're right again, but there's not a better wine in all the world. It's true. Charlie makes great wine. Superb wine."

"Can we keep walking, please?" He was getting loud and Cate worried about what the neighbors might think.

"Why of course, madam." He bowed in silence. There was very little traffic in the middle of the night, and the neighborhood took on a different feeling. She liked the peacefulness of it.

Cate yawned.

"But you're tired," he said. "Why don't you come home with me?"

"That's where we're going," she clarified.

"We are?"

"Yes, we are."

"Oh, that's good. But I don't think we can walk there. It might be too far. We better catch a plane. Do they have those around here?" He looked up and down the street as if he could catch one as it flew by.

"I don't think so."

He shrugged. "Then, we'll just have to walk."

They were two feet from the brownstone.

"We're here." Cate gently pulled him up his front stairs.

"Wow. Already. That was quick."

"It was only three blocks away."

He stopped and looked up at the brownstone, twisting his head from side to side, as if he were trying to take it all in. "But this isn't *my* house. This belongs to my parents. My house is bigger than this. And it has lots of windows. And the ocean is right outside my back door. Let's go there. It's a lot more fun. The sun shines all the time. You'll like it. It's warm. This place is too cold, and small and dark. I don't want to live here anymore. There's no sand to play in."

"Where's the key?" Cate asked, ignoring his ramblings.

He searched his pockets. "I must have lost it," he answered. "Now, let's catch that plane." He looked back down the street.

"Give me the key so I can open your door and say good-night." She held out her hand. He took it and kissed her fingers.

Suddenly, his funny-drunk demeanor changed. "Come inside with me, Cate. Stay here tonight. With me. In my bed." His voice took on a deeper tone. Cate wasn't ready for it. Had he been pretending to be drunk?

"I can't," she said without hesitation. She wasn't about to spend the night. It could be dangerous to her whole plan.

"Why?"

"Because, I just can't, that's why." She tried to pull away, but he held tight.

"Cate, I want you in my bed. It's where you belong. Where you've always belonged."

"It's Charlie's wine talking, not you."

"I don't care what it is, I only know that tonight, under these stars, and this sky, I want to make love to you. I don't care about anything else. I just know I have to have you, right now. And if I die tomorrow, then I'll die a happy man."

"Don't say that. Something might happen."

"Then let it happen, but first spend the night with me. We belong together, Cate. We always have. Please stay."

She tried to walk away, but he held on tight and pulled her toward him. He took the key out of his pocket and opened the door. This time, she let him lead her into his house.

The moonlight played on the walls, so there was no need to snap on a light. They walked straight to the bedroom, ignoring the ladders and construction litter along the way. When they got to the bedroom door he turned to her. "I'm still a little drunk, Cate, so go easy on me."

"I shouldn't do this."

"You belong with me," he said. He looked at her with a deadly serious expression. "You want to know why I left ten years ago, I'll tell you. It had absolutely nothing to do with you, believe me. I was in a panic. I had this whole vision of myself conquering the skiing world. Traveling the planet in tournaments. Living the great jock fantasy. I loved you. I've always loved you, but I also loved my dream. I understand now it was a false fear. We could have worked something out, without either of us having to give up our ambitions, but then, when you're young and stupid, you don't want anything to get in the road. Ego gets in the way of good sense. I ran. It was by far and away the dumbest and most cowardly thing I think I've ever done. I'm more than sorry. I hurt you. I humiliated you and why you are now with me is a miracle. But I'll take a miracle when it comes my way. If I can get even a little forgiveness, I'll take that as well. I love you, Cate. More than you can ever know."

She felt for a moment as if she'd lost her mind and had no idea where it was. She couldn't even talk. What could she say? He could take her right here in the damn hallway. On the planks, on the bricks, on the ladder. Her legs felt weak.

He picked her up in his arms. "Oh, my God. Take me, but do it quick before I change my mind."

Once they were inside his bedroom it was as if somebody had set a timer, everything went so fast. They kissed, and the heat of their lips sent an urgency through their bodies. There was little time for exploring or slow, sexy moves. Within minutes they were on the bed, ripping at each other's clothes and searching for the important body parts. He didn't give her time to remove her bra or get her panties all the way off before he was inside her, moving to her rhythm, like he'd never been away. Like they had been doing this for the past ten years and had gotten the moves down so well it had become second nature.

The sensations that surged through her body were incredible, and Cate tried not to think of anything else, but somehow, the wedding slipped into her mind and wouldn't let go.

"Kiss me," she told him, hoping that his kiss would tell her what was really going on in his head.

He followed her orders, and for a moment she was free from her neighborhood and free from her curse. She allowed herself to be in the moment. To feel the intensity. To feel his body, heavy on hers. To experience that *fit* they had.

That perfect *fit*.

It was at that exact moment when she felt the orgasm burn through her body and consume her with its torrent of pleasure. Rudy responded with his own release until they were both exhausted from the force of it all.

When the fire subsided, Rudy kissed her neck, her ear and her cheek, then rolled off her, wrapping his arm tightly around her waist. Cate cuddled in close, and they both lay there until Cate could hear his breathing deepen into a soft, purring rhythm.

She slowly slid off the bed, got dressed and left.

On her walk home Cate thought of only one thing, how mixed up she was over her emotions.

So, all right, this was going to be a lot harder than she'd thought. It was going to be brutal, yet she still had to do it.

But there had been a time, during their lovemaking, when her emotions had welled up to such a pitch she'd been on the verge of just confessing what this was all about, and that she was not going to go through with jilting him. But she knew she couldn't do that and possibly put him in jeopardy. If something happened to him because she didn't break the curse, she wouldn't be able to live with herself. It devastated her that she had the one she loved and had to do this to him. It would hurt her more than it could possibly hurt him. In fact, it was already hurting her now

13

CATE WOKE UP the following morning to the sound of her alarm clock, in her own bed, alone, missing Rudy. For a moment, she thought last night had been a dream, but her coat and shoes lay on the bottom of the bed where she had left them.

God, he's a good lover.

She pushed the thoughts away and refused to let them in, because every time she did, she'd get all aroused just from the memory. From the excitement of him. From the heat.

So much for celibacy.

She wanted to call him. To hear his voice.

She picked up the phone next to her bed and dialed, then hung up.

What would she say?

She dialed again.

It rang once. No answer.

The frightening thought crossed her mind that maybe Rudy had left town after all. That the wedding was too much for him.

It rang again.

Nothing.

She was just about to hang up on the third ring and berate herself for ever thinking that she could actually hold on to him long enough, when he picked up. "Hello," Rudy said into her ear.

Cate hung up. At least she knew he was at home.

Then she remembered all the amulets her mother had kept in her jewelry box that still sat on the dresser in her mother's old room. It was a room her mother had liked to go into to read or sew or just be by herself.

She got up, slipped on a fuzzy warm robe and slippers and trotted down the hallway.

The door was wide open, and as she approached she could see her father standing in the middle of the room, wearing his usual robe, hat and slippers, but staring at the far wall. Her father hadn't been inside her mother's old room since the day she was rushed to the hospital with a chest pain and never returned.

"Dad, what's wrong? Are you okay?" Cate yelled out her concerns so loud that Gina came running.

"What's wrong?" Gina said as soon as she came into the room, sleep still in her eyes.

"Dad. Say something. Tell us what to do. What's the matter?" Cate's pulse quickened at the thought that something might be wrong with her father.

"I think it's time," he said softly.

"Time for what, Dad?" Gina asked, folding her arms across her chest.

Cate held her breath.

"I think it's time to clean this room out. It's a good room, and the light, she's good on this side of the house. Your mother wouldn't like us keeping the door closed all the time, like there's something wrong with this place. It's time to move in something new. I decided—" he turned to Cate "—I decided this room needs a good woman in it again. Your mother would like that."

Cate and Gina looked at each other. What was he

mumbling on about? A good woman. Aunt Flo! Cate couldn't believe what she was seeing on her father's face. Was he actually in love? So now what are they going to do? Make it a public thing?

Cate wondered how the two of them would ever get together and stay together.

Their father came toward them and when he got to Cate, he touched her and said, "We gonna be one big happy family again, hey?" Then he kissed her forehead, and turned and kissed Gina's forehead. "I got such beautiful daughters. *Que bella familia!*" He walked out of the room, along the hallway and down the stairs, singing as he went.

"What's that all about?" Gina asked.

"I think he and Aunt Flo are coming out of the closet and into Mom's bedroom."

Gina shook her head. "Is that okay? I mean, it's our mother's room."

"They were sisters, so I guess Mom would be happy to keep him close at home."

RUDY REACHED OVER and grabbed his ringing phone from the floor next to his bed. It fell out of his hand. He opened his eyes to retrieve it, but the damn thing slipped out again. When he finally grabbed hold of it and pressed the talk button, the fool on the other end hung up.

Probably some jerk from the press.

Rudy stared at the alarm clock on the stool next to his bed. It took a while for his eyes to assimilate the time.

Damn.

It was a little past seven. He really didn't want to be

awake so early. The wedding was eight hours away. He punched down his pillow, threw the covers over his head and rolled over. Then he remembered last night and sat bolt upright.

When he thought about Cate and all that lovemaking in his bed he forgot about the paparazzi and his aches and pains. He rolled onto his back, stared at the ceiling and grinned from ear to ear. *God that woman is something.* "I'm getting married in the evening," he sang to himself. "Ding-dong the bells are gonna ring."

He felt like the luckiest man on earth.

He grabbed a blanket and slowly rolled to the side of the bed, dropped his feet on the cold, wooden floor and got up. He wanted to open the curtain and see the sun. Suddenly Taylor Street looked like it was paved with gold and that he had suddenly stumbled into paradise.

Thank you, Allison. You pushed me to my senses. You gave me back the woman I love. For that, I'll forgive you. And everybody else. Today, he said to himself, I'm going to pardon all my enemies. Well, most of them.

His doorbell rang. He ignored it, thinking it was probably the contractors.

His doorbell rang again.

Rudy got up, pulled on a pair of white pajama bottoms and went to the door. Whoever it was deserved what they got if they were going to ring his bell so early in the morning.

"Yeah. Yeah," he yelled with the fourth ring.

He opened the door, and Carmen and four of his cronies, all dressed in tuxedos, smiled at him.

"Good morning, Mr. Bellafini. We're here to help

you get ready for your wedding today," Carmen, from Carmen's Side Room, politely informed him.

"But I don't need any help, thanks," Rudy said.

He tried to close the door on the cast of *The Sopranos*, but the guy with the bulldog face and a shoulder twitch stopped him. "Sorry," he said, "but we're your groomsmen, and that's our job. It would be best if we could come in."

Another guy, who looked like your typical Hollywood mobster said, "We brought biscotti and coffee as a token of our generous nature."

They each held up little white bags as they filed into Rudy's house.

Great bunch of guys, Rudy thought. I'm going to like it around here. I'm not just gaining a wife, I'm regaining my whole community.

THERE WAS MORE FOOD in Ted's kitchen and dining room than Italy had olives, and three more platters of salads, cheese and sliced meets had just arrived at the back door.

Henry, who had returned from his honeymoon with Crying Lady Stella, couldn't help but provide a spray of pink carnations for the mantel, green calla lilies for the staircase and a huge bucket of yellow daffodils for the dining room.

Cate had decided that attempting another wedding at St. Mary's was fraught with bad memories, but there was no choice. Everybody in her world got married there. She and Aunt Flo and the dear ladies of St. Mary's bunco club decorated Cate's house for the reception.

Everything looked fabulously festive. White balloons and Hallmark pop-ups engulfed the entire house. Aunt Flo had spared no expense. She used her 40-percent employee discount.

Louie Prima's Greatest Hits filled the air, along with the constant din of conversation, Italian style.

Cate hadn't wanted a big wedding, but that wasn't possible with Florence for an aunt, so she agreed to a small celebration, immediate family and a few friends.

Aunt Flo had other ideas.

The simple wedding had turned into a reason for cousins to fly in from Genoa, Naples and Cariati Marina, and one estranged great-aunt flew in from Argentina, Lucille Marie Nudi. Lucille spoke no English, but played a mean accordion, something every good Italian wedding needed. Then there was cousin Gusti from Wisconsin who played the classical guitar, and second cousin Bernie from Indiana. He played the mandolin and, well, the list went on and on.

It seemed that it was good luck for everyone to attend a revenge wedding, at least that's what Aunt Flo had said.

"But I thought the revenge part was a secret?" Cate asked her aunt as she sat in front of the dresser mirror in her bedroom.

Rose Marie stood behind Cate, putting the finishing touches on her perfectly styled hair, while Gina slipped on a bridesmaid dress in the corner. "Oh, no," Rose Marie said. "You can't keep a thing like this a secret, or else how are you gonna get your revenge? The more people who know the better. This is a good thing you're doing, Cate. It's good luck for everybody." She stopped fussing, came around and leaned on the dresser to look at Cate. "So, when ya gonna do it?

When you walk down the aisle? No. Maybe right when Father Joe says that part about 'Is there anybody here...'? No, that might not be a good time, either. Ya know, I think I'd do it during the vows, myself. Right when everybody's waiting for you to say 'I do,' you say 'I don't.' Oh, I like that one, don't you?" She nudged Cate on her shoulder and laughed.

"What's wrong with everybody around here? Is there no sense of empathy for the groom?" Cate asked indignantly.

"What empathy?" Rose Marie retorted. "He's a louse. It's guys like him that give the rest of his gender a bad name."

"Rudy is not a louse," Cate protested. "He can be really sweet."

"They all can, dearie. As long as they're getting what they want, if you know what I mean." She pumped her hips a few times for affect.

Cate thought, What about when the girl is getting what she wants! The thought gave her goose bumps.

Aunt Flo said, "Let's not dwell on that. Let's be happy. This is a happy occasion."

"Yeah, for everybody else," Cate said. "Where's my happiness? When do I get to be happy?" Can I really go through with this? she wondered.

"Don't worry so much, doll. These things take time."

"Yeah, well, I'm running out of time."

"You're young. You got your whole life ahead of you."

"I'm not so young." She leaned in closer to the mirror. "Look at me. Look at those lines around my eyes, and I'm getting a double chin already. Look at that."

She turned sideways so her aunt could get a better look.

Aunt Flo dug around in her Marilyn Monroe purse, which sat on the floor next to the dresser, pulled out a pack of gum and displayed it in her hands. "If you chew three or four sticks a day, it'll keep your chin fat tight. I prefer Orbit sugarless, myself. It also helps fight tooth decay and bad breath. Plus, it's very refreshing."

Cate took the pack of gum, ripped it open, pulled one out, shoved it into her mouth and started chewing.

Her aunt was right. She could feel her chin fat tightening up already.

"ARE YOU READY?" Gina asked Cate as the two women stood in the room that connected the rectory with the church. They were the only two left in the room.

Cate had just fastened her mother's small coral horn around her neck to ward off any evil eyes that might look her way.

"I think so," Cate answered after taking in a deep cleansing breath to calm her ever-present nerves. This should have happened ten years ago, but she understood now why he'd fled. The thing that really bothered her was that her mother couldn't be here now to see. But then, what did it matter. This wasn't going to be real. This was a revenge wedding, so maybe it was better that her mother didn't see it.

Cate felt confused and distraught. She so wanted this moment, yet not this way and for this reason. God, she hated doing this to Rudy, even if everyone in her world thought he deserved it, and even if it was necessary to break the curse.

"You *think* or you're sure?"

"I'm sure, I guess."

"That doesn't sound too positive to me. You want to talk about this?"

"It's too late for talk. I'm in a white dress. Father Joe is ready and Great-Aunt Lucille is playing the wedding march."

"And she plays it quite well, I might add." They could hear the accordion music through the closed door. Great-Aunt Lucille had brought along her own sound system.

"I just wanted to talk to Rudy before the wedding, but I couldn't bring myself to call him. He's out there, right?"

"Yes, standing right next to Vinney at the front of the church, along with five other guys I've never seen before."

Cate cringed. "Does one of them look like Elvis?"

"Yes. You know these guys?"

"They're like cousins."

"And what about the five bridesmaids?"

"More cousins."

"Our family's too big. If I ever have kids, I'm only having one."

Cate sighed as Gina handed her the bride's bouquet made up of white calla lilies with a gold ribbon. Gina wore a gold satin gown that Mrs. Crocetti had left over from another wedding when one of the bridesmaids' pregnancy bloomed quicker than the dress had seams.

Gina was radiant, of course. The gold satin only enhanced her deep-olive skin, and the lines of the dress accentuated her tiny, perfect figure.

Cate, on the other hand, thought for sure she looked almost sinful in her tasteful, but backless halter wedding gown. Gina had picked it out and Mrs. Crocetti had discounted the dress for good luck.

Cate grabbed the doorknob, ready to open the door.

Gina said, "Let's take a second and hit the highlights."

Cate let go of the doorknob.

"You're doing this revenge wedding because..."

"Because I don't want anything bad to happen to anybody else."

"And?"

"And, this is the only way to break the curse."

"And?"

"And, because my last fiancé nearly choked to death on a canolli."

"Makes perfect sense to me, but are you happy?"

"No."

"Great. Everything's as it should be."

Aunt Flo burst into the room. "What's the holdup, dolls? We got over a hundred people out there waiting for the bride. Aunt Lucille's fingers are getting numb. Are you going to walk up the aisle to jilt him now?"

"Tell her to start the music one more time. I'm coming down," Cate told her aunt.

Aunt Flo stepped out of the room and yelled, "*Cominciare!* Hit it, Lucille."

She stepped back in, winked at Cate and said, "Go get 'em, baby doll."

Cate fluffed out her veil, stood up straight, poised her bouquet and walked to where her father, looking rather handsome in his rented tuxedo, stood at the doors leading into the church, waiting for her to take his arm.

"Cate," her father said, "you look like an angel from

Heaven. Your mother is looking down and she's smiling and proud. Such a day."

Cate glanced at herself in the door's glass and was surprised that she did indeed look very bridelike. Angelic. Pure. Virginal. Looks can be so deceiving, she thought.

EVERYONE MADE little "ah" sounds as Cate came into view.

Father Joe patiently waited at the altar with his missal poised for the ceremony.

Vinney and the five groomsmen smiled at Cate.

The five bridesmaids, dressed in matching green dresses, also smiled at Cate and Gina.

The bank of invited press began snapping pictures.

All Cate had to do was walk right down the aisle and right out the side door and away from the love of her life. She didn't know if she could do it, curse or no curse. Equally, she feared the consequences if she didn't.

Each step brought added misery and tension.

14

RUDY WATCHED as Cate took her father's arm and began their slow walk toward him, toward their future together. She looked almost unreal, like something from a dream, the flowing white gown, the halter top fitting her perfectly. God, he thought, she's amazing, and she's mine.

But as she drew closer he noticed something was wrong with her expression. The lovely bride wasn't staring longingly at the awaiting groom.

She was staring at the side door.

Cate didn't seem interested in him or in what was happening, instead she seemed fixated on that door. It looked to him as if she was thinking hard about something, or concentrating, planning even.

When she was about ten feet away from Rudy, she suddenly bolted.

What the hell! Rudy thought.

Some people were actually cheering and clapping!

Rudy stared in disbelief as his bride began to run. Gina ran ahead of her and opened the side door. Cate quickly turned toward him and he thought she mouthed something like "I'm sorry." Then the two women vanished behind the door.

"What's happening?" Rudy said, turning to Vinney.

"Looks like cold feet to me."

"What?"

"People get cold feet." Vinney shrugged.

"Vinney!"

"The curse, man, the curse."

"What the hell are you talking about?"

"That's how the curse has to be broken. You jilted her, now she jilted you. It's the only way the curse could be broken," Vinney said. "Man, you put it on her, now you took it off."

"I don't believe this."

"Believe, cause it's true."

"You people are all crazy."

Rudy watched the people filing out. Some of them were congratulating Ted, slapping him on the back. Aunt Flo looked positively buoyant.

The press was going crazy taking pictures.

Rudy said, "You mean to tell me that all these people were in on it?"

"You need to talk to Flo. Yeah, we all knew."

Rudy couldn't believe everyone would go to all this trouble to get even. He was angry. This was nuts. He'd apologized, hadn't he? They'd made love, hadn't they?

The idea that she had used him, had played his emotions, *lured* him! All the time just setting him up for this. The whole world would hear about this. It would destroy his reputation. Make a laughingstock out of him.

He stared at the now-empty church, shaking his head. He looked at Father Joe. "Was I that bad that I deserved this?"

"A woman scorned, my boy." He patted Rudy on the arm and walked away.

Rudy stared after him. *Et tu Brute*, Rudy thought.

At that moment the paparazzi broke in through the

front of the church. They swarmed around him yelling and snapping pictures. He grabbed a camera that had been pushed in his face, turned and got smacked with another one. A shuffle ensued. Finally he broke free when Father Joe came in and kicked them all out.

"I DID IT!" Cate said, holding her throbbing eye shut as she and Gina ran out the door with four media guys close on their heels, snapping pictures. "I broke my curse. I'm a free woman." Cate wanted to feel ecstatic, free, triumphant, but she didn't.

"Are you happy now?" Gina asked as they made their way to the waiting limo across the lawn.

"I had to do it, but no, I'm not happy about it."

"What's wrong?"

"I hit my face on the door."

"Are you all right?"

"I guess so."

"Well, you're even now. If you get back with him, it'll be on even ground."

"*If* is the operative word. He's not going to take this any better than I did. I doubt I'll ever see him again after this. It'll be all over the papers and on TV. He's going to hate me."

With the help of the driver, the two women stepped into the back of the waiting limo. It was a plush car, with black leather seats, chrome appointments and thick gray carpet. An open bottle of champagne sat ready for the first toast, while Tony Bennett and B.B. King sang "Let The Good Times Roll" on the CD player.

Everything was perfect. As it should be. All was right with the world. Except Cate was miserable. But then, whacking your head on a hard surface, not to mention losing the love of your life, will do that to a person.

RUDY SNUCK OUT through the rectory with the help of Father Joe and made his way back to the brownstone to nurse his bloody nose.

He went to his bedroom to pack his things and get out on the next flight. But instead of packing he walked to the window and looked out at Taylor Street.

It amazed him that an entire community could be involved in something like this. He stared at the Italian American Sports Hall of Fame. How could these people do this to a favorite son? I've brought them glory and this is what I get in return? Just because I jilted a girl? What's wrong with these people?

But then he thought about it from their perspective—from her family's perspective—and he started to see where they were coming from. Everyone had been building up to that wedding day ten years ago. He was an athlete with promise and Italians love their athletes. She was the smartest and prettiest girl in town, with that magic touch and everyone loved her.

Okay, so walking out was not a good thing. It was a bad thing, but was it that bad? Apparently so. Now he could see how devastated her family and friends had been. How angry the whole town was. He'd jilted not just her but all of them. Led them down the garden path and then snubbed them. Too good for her, for them. That's what they probably thought.

And maybe, just maybe, they were right. It wasn't a justifiable act. He should have been straight with her, with everybody. And having his mother tell her that he'd left! That was really low.

What now? Run away again. That's what everyone expects, he thought. *Well, this time they're wrong. I'm not running away.*

But there was a very big question that needed answering. Was she faking everything or did she really love him? He wasn't leaving until he knew the truth about that one.

"YOU HAVE TO HOLD the ice right on it, or it's going to turn yellow," Gina told her sister. The three women were in Aunt Flo's apartment, still wearing their wedding dresses. Cate was sprawled out on the sofa while Gina sat on the floor next to her. Cate followed Gina's orders and pressed the zipped baggie tight against her right eye.

Aunt Flo said, "A steak would be better. Draws the pain right out like a sponge. I got a nice sirloin tip that was made for that eye."

"How does it look?" Cate asked as she removed the baggie.

Her sister flinched and made a face.

"That bad, huh?"

Cate could feel her eye throb with each beat of her heart. It wasn't so bad when she was lying down and keeping her eye closed. It only killed her when she tried to get up.

"Now what?" Cate moved the bag to her forehead. To compound matters, she was getting a headache. "Is it all over?"

"Not yet, doll. You have to do what he did."

Cate sat up. "What?"

"He dated every pretty girl he could find. Well, that's what you're going to do."

"She has to date every pretty girl around?" Gina asked.

"This isn't funny, Gina," Aunt Flo chastised. "She has to date every eligible guy around. Then she'll be even."

"Aunt Flo is right," Gina said. "You need some intense dating with several guys to clean the slate. And if they don't have accidents, choke on their steaks or get run over by trucks, then we know you're free. It's the only way."

Dating other men was the last thing in the world she wanted to do. "I don't want to. I think the curse is off now. The jilt was enough."

"Then why do you have a black eye?" Gina asked.

"She's right," Aunt Flo added. "There can only be one reason."

They both turned and looked at her.

"You're still in love with Rudy Bellafini. I told you not to count your chickens."

"I am not."

"I think you are. I never heard of this happening before, but I'm almost sure you can't be free of the curse if you're still in love with him."

"But I am free of him. I did everything I was supposed to do."

Aunt Flo shook her head. "I got a feeling this thing ain't over. The dating will tell a lot. It'll prove it one way or another...I think."

"If nothing happens to them?"

"Yeah, that's it. And maybe you'll get a sign of some sort. If you can fall for another man it will prove you are finally free of Rudy, free to find another love. True love is committed. True love is forever. I never heard of a woman going through with a revenge wedding and still loving the guy. This is a new one. Rudy might even be cursed now."

Cate moved the ice back to her eye. She didn't know which hurt more. And now her neck began to tighten up. Somehow this was not the vision she had when she was a kid and she dreamed about her love life.

"And who's going to date me when I look like this? I need a mirror. Can someone please give me a mirror?"

Gina got up to find one. Aunt Flo told her where to look.

"Minor details. I know a nice boy from Marshall Fields. I'll set you up. He won't know nothing about this curse," Aunt Flo said.

"It'll be all over the newspapers tomorrow." Cate pressed her free hand into the back of her neck.

"With that eye, who's gonna recognize you?"

"I found the mirror," Gina said.

Cate took it and looked at her eye. Her skin had turned a ridiculous shade of yellow, and a deep-blue color encircled her entire eyelid. Her eyeball itself was completely bloodshot, not to mention all the swelling. Tears welled up as she looked at herself in the small hand mirror.

"Don't cry, doll. It'll make your good eye puffy."

Cate let out a loud wail.

"PUT YOUR HEAD BACK," Vinney ordered Rudy as the two men stood in Rudy's bathroom trying to get his bloody nose under control. Vinney had stopped by to check on Rudy just as the three women stormed out of his brownstone.

"Damn paparazzi attacked me," Rudy said.

Vinney handed him ice cubes wrapped in a white hand towel. "Here, put this on your nose."

Rudy looked at Vinney. "Dude, it feels like it might be broken."

Vinney surveyed Rudy's nose. "No. If it was broken, it'd be a balloon by now, and your eyes would be black-and-blue."

"I can't believe this," Rudy muttered. The bleeding had partially subsided so the two men walked out of the bathroom and into the living room. There were only two pieces of furniture. Rudy sat down on the couch. Vinney took the green leather recliner.

"That's going to be sore for a couple days."

Rudy looked at Vinney. "You are the one guy I wouldn't have thought would keep me in the dark about this."

"I live here, man. And don't forget, I once dated Cate and a tree fell on me, damned near killed me. I have a vested interest in this thing going to the end."

Rudy shook his head but quickly stopped. It just made his nose start bleeding again.

"You got to admire what she did," Vinney said.

"I do?"

"She pulls that off against a famous guy like you, all the press around. Took some guts for her to go through with it. Besides, I think she likes you a lot more than she puts on. Not that she should, being what you did to her and all."

"Yeah, you're right. She's the best."

"So, like, what are you going to do now?"

"That depends on what's next. Is this curse thing over or what?"

"I'm not sure what the end is. Could be over. Maybe there's more. They don't tell me everything. Look at your nose. That don't look to me like it's completely over. I'd be careful."

GINA, AUNT FLO AND CATE were getting ready for bed when there was a loud knock at the door. Gina went and opened it, and for a second Cate thought it might be an angry Rudy. Instead it was Vinney. He came rushing in like he had big news. "I thought I'd find you guys here. I just came from Rudy's and I thought you should know, he's had an accident."

"What!" they all yelled in unison.

"No, not bad. Just smashed his nose up a bit. We got the bleeding stopped. I don't think it's broken or nothin'. But as soon as I saw it, I thought Aunt Flo should know." He looked at Cate. "What happened to you?"

"She hit a door on the way out of the church," Gina said.

The three women stared at him. He stared back.

"Well, I've got to get going. I'm on duty for the next three days. Just wanted to let you know."

They watched him leave and then Cate and Gina turned to Aunt Flo. She shrugged. "Well, I guess we know for sure now. You and Rudy both got the curse."

Cate was determined to break this thing, especially now that Rudy had it, too. Something worse than a bloody nose could happen to him, then how would she feel? She had to work fast. "What do I have to do?"

"You gotta go out like I said and date other men. If

you get past that, then, doll, you gotta look Rudy square in those beautiful eyes of his and tell him from your heart that you don't love him no more."

"Will it be over then?"

"Pretty much."

"'Pretty much'? What does that mean?"

"Why do you always gotta ask questions? I'm telling you everything I know. These things are complicated. Now get some sleep, doll. You'll feel better in the morning."

Cate went off to bed, but Gina and Aunt Flo stayed behind for a moment.

"Is this really going to work?" Gina asked once Cate was out of earshot.

"I can't be sure of anything, now that they love each other."

"Then why did you tell her all that 'look him in the eye' stuff?"

"It's the best I can do. They gotta figure out they love each other on their own, and maybe the curse will go away. When you love somebody, you can't tell them that you don't love them. It's impossible. So, maybe this will help get them back together. I just want what's best for my two dolls."

Gina opened her arms and they hugged.

"I know," Gina said, resting her head on Aunt Flo's shoulder.

"Let's get some sleep. I gotta look good for all them single guys I haveta set up for your sister."

15

IT HAD BEEN a long day...a long week, a long couple of weeks, and Cate was ready to say good-night to Kenny Stover, the last of Aunt Flo's blind dates from Marshall Fields. Cate had dated a guy in Shoes, another from Menswear, Pete from Boyswear, Ben from Fine Jewelry and Joe from Cosmetics, who was in the middle of a sex change, so he didn't count.

Now Aunt Flo had run out of department store men, and was considering branching out to the sons of the ladies of St. Mary's bunco club. That's when Cate put the skids on the whole dating experiment. Aunt Flo had a simple philosophy: if they were single, they were a perfect date for Cate. Amazingly, there had been some really great guys, but she didn't feel anything for any of them, yet. It will take time, she kept telling herself. Give them a chance. If they don't fall down an elevator shaft, and could kiss and make her feel it, she would be home free.

So it was going to be Kenny Stover—blind date number six. He was hot. All the girls at the Marshall Fields wanted the guy.

She had conducted each of her dates in the same manner, and by the end of the evening, she would say the exact same thing, and her date would take the bait. Kenny would be no exception.

"I love the view from the top of the Sears Tower,

don't you?" They were just coming out of a Starbucks near the tower.

She had dragged each of her dates, including Kenny, through revolving doors, climbed dozens of stairs, taken trains, buses and cabs, and even sat up front during Blackhawks hockey games, and nothing. None of them had fallen, tripped or even burped. A puck came right for date number three—Ben from Fine Jewelry—at a hundred miles an hour, and Ben ducked.

"Not really. I don't like heights."

"What?"

"The Sears Tower. I can't go up there. It plugs up my ears and I hate that feeling."

"But it's so romantic," she whispered, desperately trying for her final test.

He smiled. "Sure, why not."

Well, she thought, he's willing to take chances. My kind of guy. So up they went in the elevator, her arm in his, just like a couple of old lovers. Maybe this was the one. The curse breaker extraordinaire. Good looking. Dresses well. Keeps in shape. He's the manager of Women's Shoes and on the rise. Free trendy shoes for life! What more could a girl want? And curly hair!

So there they were, with a 360 view of Chicago. She snuggled up against him. Turned and looked up at him, giving him that come-kiss-me gaze. He gazed into her eyes and leaned in. He said, "You know, your aunt Flo is something. She makes me laugh all the time. One time—"

She couldn't wait, so she pulled him to her. They kissed. She waited. Nothing. She kissed him again, this time with determination. He tried but it just wasn't there. No heat. No magic. His lips were too thin.

Don't be judgmental, she told herself. Not everybody has all of Rudy's experience with kissing. Not everybody can melt you on the first kiss. Give this guy at least half a chance.

But it just didn't work out. She tried twice more. Once when they were walking past the Art Institute and once more at the car. Nope. Not happening. No spark. No nothing.

"So," he said, "is it true that Bellafini slugged you?"

"What? Where did you hear that?"

"Somebody said so in one of the tabloids."

"No, that's not true. You can't believe anything they write. I'm an active kind of girl. Accidents seem to happen to me all the time."

"That explains the black eye, then," he said skeptically.

"It's almost healed," she said, thinking she had covered it with makeup.

"So, it didn't happen that way, then. That's what I told Pete, that he wasn't the kind of guy who would slug women. You went out with Pete last Thursday night."

"It was last Friday night, actually."

"Yeah. Whatever. Anyway, I told him not to believe everything he reads in those newspapers about you and your ex-fiancé."

Cate was disappointed, but what's a girl to do?

When they finally parted company back at her front door, she avoided another awkward Kenny kiss and said good-night. Kenny ran across the street to his car.

Tires squealed.

Normally, she'd be waiting for the sound of crashing metal. Then an ambulance. Not this time. She knew he'd be just as safe as the other five dates. Accidents were no longer the problem.

The dating experiment had proved that the curse was off the men she dated. The problem was, she saw no hope of falling for any of them. And, according to Aunt Flo, that had to happen because she couldn't be in love with Rudy or the curse would never be lifted.

It's ridiculous that I'm so hung up on this guy, she thought. *Time. Maybe it's just a matter of time. Keep away from him.*

No, time hadn't worked before, and it certainly wasn't going to work now.

Stop thinking about him, she told herself. *Stop acting like a silly schoolgirl and grow up. You don't love Rudy Bellafini. You can't love him. Say it out loud, with some conviction. Do it for Rudy's sake. C'mon, coward, yell it to the neighborhood.*

"I don't love Rudy Bellafini," she said in an anemic voice.

Louder!

"I don't love Rudy Bellafini!"

Better. Once more and make it real.

"I love—I don't love Rudy—"

"Hey, lady, we don't care. Go to bed!" somebody yelled back.

Cate sighed, turned around and went inside.

It HAD BEEN A WEEK since Cate's last date, and she had absolutely refused any more of Aunt Flo's department store Romeos.

She was going back into the celibacy mode, at least for the time being. She pulled a brown throw tighter around her shoulders as she relaxed on the sofa. Her dad sat next to her in his recliner.

"A skunk is always a skunk." Her dad said, while simultaneously reading the paper and watching TV, upset about something she wasn't paying any attention to.

She'd seen Rudy only twice, both times from a distance and each time she'd wanted to go and talk to him. Be with him. She was sure he knew all about the curse and her actions from Vinney, and everyone else in the neighborhood, but she wanted to tell him herself. Yet she knew she couldn't. She wished he would just go, and then maybe she could stop thinking about him. Get over this thing she had for the guy.

"Why aren't you out with Aunt Flo tonight?" Cate shoved a small red pillow under her head.

"I can't find her. Why aren't you out on a date?"

She only had one answer for that question. "I need a break from boring guys."

"Now that the curse is broken, you should be out mingling. How are you ever gonna get married if you don't mingle?" He turned the page on his *Sun Times* and straightened out the paper with a flourish.

"How are you ever going to get married if you can't find Aunt Flo?" She turned to face her father.

"Who said anything about getting married?" He folded up part of the paper and threw it down next to the chair.

"You did, the day of my wedding."

"No, I didn't."

"You said we were all going to be one happy family."

"Maybe I did, but she don't want to marry me." He opened another section and started skimming.

"Did you ask her?"

"No. If I could find her, I'd ask, but who can find a woman who moves around so much?" He looked over at Cate.

She thought for a moment. "Why don't you invite her over for dinner?"

"She won't come because she thinks I'm asking her out on a date."

"Then I'll ask her, and you can just be here."

"She'll think you set up a date, and she'll leave."

Agitation set in as Cate tossed around on the sofa, trying to get comfortable. "How are you two ever going to get together like this?"

He shrugged. "Maybe I'll run into her at the A&P tomorrow and I'll ask her there."

"You can't ask Aunt Flo to marry you in a grocery store." Cate sat up.

"Why not? It's a new store. The lighting's good and they got an Italian deli. I can ask her while she's buying a pound of cheese. That way she won't think it's a date."

"Dad, do you know how crazy this sounds?"

"Could be, but what else am I gonna do?"

Cate thought about it, and he was right. The deli aisle at the A&P was the perfect place for a marriage proposal, especially in this family.

"I'm going to bed," she announced, imagining Rudy waiting for her, naked, smiling, as she stood up to leave.

"I'm gonna stay up for a little more. That sister of yours ain't home yet."

"She's a big girl, Dad."

"Not to me she ain't."

She kissed him on the cheek and left the room, envisioning her dad kneeling in front of a glass case of cold cuts asking Aunt Flo to be his bride. She could only hope she said yes, or her poor father would never be able to buy a pound of salami again.

"You MADE THE COVER," Gina said, as they stood in the waiting room in front of a small reception desk. There were three patients using the machines, and one more patient waited inside a private room. Business at the Wellness Center had picked up, but the noise coming from the construction crew next door made it hard for everyone to concentrate.

Cate grabbed the magazine out of her sister's hand to get a better look, and sure enough, there she was in the lower-right corner of *Celebrity Magazine*, running out of St. Mary's church. More photos and the full story continued on page fifty-six.

Cate handed the publication back to her sister.

"You'd think we were the hottest stars around. Our whole wedding fiasco has been over for three weeks and I still can't go to the Loop without somebody stopping me on the street to shake my hand. This is only going to make it worse. Isn't there some other scandal happening in Hollywood? Do they have to come to Chicago for their cover page?"

"You agreed to let them do the story."

"They caught me when I was down."

"Literally."

"I can't imagine why they would be interested in some guy and girl having a simple dispute."

"But it's not just any guy, Cate. It's the playboy of the decade."

"I wouldn't say the decade. Besides, the past is over."

"Then you won't care that he bought Mr. McCafferty's old building next door."

Her sister's statement knocked the wind right out of Cate's cocky sails. "He did not."

"Did, too."

"Is that what all that noise is about?"

"It's right here on page fifty-six—'Rudy Bellafini told *Celebrity* that he intends to stay put for a while and call Little Italy his home again. He plans to open an even bigger restaurant than any of his others, and help turn Little Italy into the tourist attraction it deserves to be.'"

Cate didn't like this new aspect of the situation. Was this a publicity stunt he worked out with his "people" to get back at her? Then, the instant she thought that, she reminded herself it was good. It would make her angry with him. Help in the process of getting him out of her system.

Gina checked on the patients using the Nautilus machines while Cate tried to understand Rudy's motive for moving in next door. She had thought that by now he would have certainly moved on.

Before Cate could get back to work, a UPS driver walked in with a delivery. She signed for it, and he left. It was from Rudy.

She had a curious pang of apprehension when she read his name on the label.

She tore open the outer box and pulled out some wrappings. There was another box inside. She carefully opened it and inside was the most beautiful single strand of white-gold and diamonds she had ever seen. And then she remembered that day ten years ago in the back of his dad's restaurant when he'd proposed. It gave her goose bumps. Obviously, he was trying to woo her. She simply couldn't let that happen. It was way too risky for both of them, especially Rudy. He didn't understand the curse and couldn't ward off the accidents like she could.

The small card simply said: "Love, Rudy."

The noise from the renovations next door increased, and Cate just couldn't take it another minute. She had to be strong for both their sakes. Besides, she had a clinic filled with patients and had to get back to work.

"This has got to stop," Cate said out loud. She grabbed the box with the necklace and marched out of her office.

Getting in to see Rudy proved to be almost impossible. "I'm sorry, but Mr. Bellafini will be in meetings all day, and unless you have an appointment, he won't be able to see you, Ms.... what did you say your name was?" the tall, twenty-something blonde asked. She sat behind a large black desk in the front office on the top floor. The restaurant would undoubtedly take up the entire bottom floor.

"I didn't say," Cate told her.

"Well, if you want to leave me your name, I'll try and get you in. Let's see." She pulled up something on the ultrathin monitor in front of her. "I can get you an appointment with Mr. Bellafini at eleven-thirty on the twenty-third of next month, but it's just an introductory slot for fifteen minutes. If you want anything longer, you'll have to wait for at least three months. Will that be all right?"

She looked up and pasted on a smile. Her hands were perched in midair waiting to type in the appointment.

"I don't want an appointment. I want the noise to stop. You're disturbing my patients."

"I'm sorry, but the construction noise is kept at a level that's within the guidelines of the local authorities. If you have a problem with their guidelines, I suggest you take it up with them."

Cate wanted to scream, but even if she did, no one would hear her. She decided to use another tactic. "Tell you what, I'm Cate Falco. Does that make a difference?"

The woman jumped up from her chair as if she was on a spring. "Oh. It's you. Yes. You can go right in. Follow me."

Cate followed her into a plush office. The room was decorated in ultramodern black chairs and a black desk, creamy white walls, with tan carpeting and a lavender sofa. Rudy sat behind the desk. When he saw it was Cate, he jumped up. "Cate!" His gaze immediately went to the box, and a big smile appeared on his face.

The blonde left, closing the door behind her.

Cate slid the necklace box across his empty desk. "What is this?" she asked.

"A wedding present. The groom always gives the bride a wedding present."

"We never made it that far, remember?"

"It's for our future wedding."

Cate let out a sarcastic little chuckle. "You can't be serious."

"Perfectly."

"Oh, come on. Our wedding days are over. Give it to your secretary."

"She's married with two kids."

"That never stopped you before."

"I never wanted to be married before."

"Don't let it go to your head. It's temporary."

"Cate, please take the necklace." He slid it back to her. "Consider it a gift for everything I've put you through."

She slid it back all the way over to his side of the desk.

"Thanks, but I don't want it. We're even now. The curse is broken. We can't be together."

"Look, let's just talk about this. About us. About where we can go from here."

She didn't want to do this anymore. "It doesn't matter. It's over. I'm only here because of the noise. I can hear everything next door. It's bad for my patients."

"Do you have any patients right now?"

"Yes."

"I'll take care of it in a minute. God, it's good to see you. You look great. I heard about the black eye. I'm sorry."

"Thanks."

"How about if we grab a coffee someplace?"

"Thanks, but I have to get back."

Aunt Flo was right. In order to get this whole thing over with, she was going to have to look him in the eye and tell him. But he had such fabulous eyes.

"Can I call you sometime?"

"Please don't," she said while gazing down at his desk.

"I'll take care of the noise."

"Thanks," she mumbled, and turned and walked out of his office.

RUDY STARED at the closed door for a long time after Cate left. He tapped his fingers on the necklace box. He had thought for sure she was still in love with him, so why was she fighting it so hard? Dating all those guys?

He wasn't ready to accept that she'd moved on. He couldn't accept it. He acknowledged with a wry inward grin and a shake of his head that the tables had turned. Now she was out dating the world while he sat at home, pining.

But her returning the necklace had thrown him off balance for a moment.

He reached for the phone.

"Henry, just the guy I want to talk to."

16

JUST AS CATE was closing up the clinic for the night, Henry appeared at her front door looking all clean and shiny, like he had just stepped out of a shower and put on his brand-new clothes just for her. "Hi Henry. It's nice to see you."

"You, too, Cate." He stood as if waiting for her to invite him in.

"I'm closed for the day, Henry. But if you call tomorrow, I'm sure I can fit you in somewhere."

"Oh, no. Nothing like that. I saw the light, and Stella and I thought we should stop by to ask you to dinner."

He sounded as if he were repeating rehearsed lines. And the way he just stood there, grinning, was enough to give Cate the willies.

Maybe she was just tired.

"Thanks, Henry, but it's been a long day."

"You have to eat. Please. My lovely wife and I would be honored to have you join us." He nodded over to a black Ford Escape parked next to the curb. All Cate could see was a hand waving out of the car window.

Cate couldn't justify turning him down, after all, she had nearly killed him with a canolli. The least she could do was accept his dinner invitation.

"Sure, Henry. I'd love to. Just let me get my things."

Henry walked off to his Escape while Cate slipped on her coat, grabbed her purse and locked the front door. Actually, she found herself looking forward to dinner. It was her chance to apologize to poor Henry for all her evil deeds.

Cate opened the back door of the Escape and stepped up to get inside when someone reached out to help her. She grabbed hold before she could see who it was, assuming that even Henry was scheming to set her up on a blind date.

"Hi, Cate," Rudy said, while holding onto her hand.

She let go. "It's you."

"None other."

She sat back in her seat and stared at Rudy for a moment. Then she turned to Henry as he started up the street. "Henry, why didn't you tell me Rudy was in the car?"

"But I saw you wave. Didn't you wave to Rudy?"

"I waved to your wife."

Stella turned around, waved and giggled.

Cate turned her attention back to Rudy. "I told you we were through."

He smiled at her and she could see that sly twinkle in his eye. She knew what he was up to, but it wouldn't work.

In fact, she thought, maybe it was a good time to tell him that our staying apart was for his own good. Use this awkward night to set him straight. Clear the air. Get him to realize the threat he's under...we're both under.

Henry parked at Carmen's Side Room. Cate smiled. Rudy was going all out. But he wasn't going to win no matter what he did.

The restaurant was alive with laughter and conversation. Carmen escorted them to the back of the restaurant, next to the very table she and Rudy had sat at just a few weeks before. She couldn't help but reflect on how much had changed since then.

"If he gives you any problems, Cate, just let me know, and me and the boys will take care of him," Carmen told Cate while looking straight at Rudy.

"I think I can handle him," Cate said. Carmen nodded, but gave Rudy a hard look.

"I don't think he likes me," Rudy whispered in her ear.

"He likes you. He's just not a jovial kind of guy."

"So what does he look like when he's really angry?"

"You don't want to know."

Carmen pulled out Cate's chair, which was next to Rudy's and across from Henry's. Stella grinned over at Henry, while Henry gazed back at Stella with his usual startled expression. Rudy stared at his menu, while Carmen walked back to the bar, then sat down on a stool and turned to watch their table.

Cate had to admit, this was already one strange evening, but she felt good about it. Sure, Rudy had a voice she'd always loved listening to, a great sense of humor, and was about the best-looking man around, but none of that mattered. She didn't care. She was on a mission to control her emotions, and no matter what happened, she was going to succeed. Even if she did need a couple drinks to manage it.

Once the entrees were ordered and the white wine was poured, Henry leaned in with his glass in midair. "I want to propose a toast," he said. "To two of the best people on the planet. Without you two, Stella and I would never have had the chance to fall in love and get married."

Everyone clinked glasses and drank.

But there was more. "I've been doing a lot of thinking, and I'm glad I almost died."

Cate swallowed hard. The wine stung as it went down.

"No offense, Cate, but you were never the girl for me. You're not my type. Stella's my girl, and I would have never known that if I didn't nearly choke to death on that canolli."

"I don't know what to say, Henry," Cate said, thinking that the man must be crazy in love with his wife to be that happy over nearly dying.

"Just be happy for us," he said, and leaned over and kissed Stella. It was a sweet kiss. "And to Rudy. His generosity knows no bounds."

Crying Lady Stella held her hand up to her mouth, but she only let out a walloping chuckle.

AS THE EVENING PROGRESSED, and Rudy became more relaxed now that Carmen had busied himself with his restaurant, Rudy couldn't take his eyes off Cate: the way she moved, the way she spoke, her smile. He loved to just sit and watch her as she glided through each conversation with an ease that was all Cate.

A Dean Martin song played in the background, "All I Do Is Dream of You," and Rudy had a sudden desire to hold her in his arms.

"Dance with me, Cate," Rudy said.

She looked over at him and smirked. "But you don't know how."

"I can fake it. Come on." He held out his hand. She was reluctant. "Just one dance."

When she took his hand so he could lead her to the

dance floor, he felt as though he had somehow won one in his favor. And when he took her in his arms, he knew it was a terrific beginning. Then as he slowly twirled her around, a feeling of total self-confidence washed over him.

Until he twirled her again and then tried to bring her in tight against him. She came in close and he looked into her eyes, and that's when she stepped on his foot, hard.

"Rudy, I'm sorry. Are you all right?"

The hot pain shot up from his big toe. He tried to smile. "Yes. It's fine. Fine. Don't worry about it." He had the distinct feeling she'd done that deliberately.

They started dancing again. He was more careful this time when he twirled her. Then he accidentally stepped on her foot. They were suddenly getting very clumsy. He was leading in one direction; she seemed to always want to go in another.

"I guess you're right about the dancing."

"I think we should sit down," she said, and limped off the floor.

All through the meal she ignored him, didn't laugh at his jokes and acted as if he wasn't there. The night was a complete bust. It was almost like she was deliberately trying to prove something.

Whatever it is, Rudy thought, it's not going to work.

"HELLO," CATE SAID into her cell phone, fearing it was Rudy.

It was late on a Saturday afternoon, her work week was over and all Cate wanted to do was lounge around the house and maybe read a book to escape her peculiar life.

"You gotta come to St. Mary's right now. And bring your sister," Cate's dad whispered over the phone.

"Dad, are you all right? I can hardly hear you."

"Don't ask questions. Just get your sister and come down here right now."

The phone went silent.

She refused to panic as she phoned Gina. "We're supposed to go to St. Mary's. Dad phoned."

"When?"

"Now."

"I'll meet you there."

Cate and Gina arrived at the same time, and when they walked into the church their dad met them at the door.

"Your aunt should come through here any minute," he said, wringing his hands and nervously wiping the sweat from his forehead.

Cate put her arm around her father's shoulder. "What's this all about, Dad? Why are we here?"

"I can't say. Just sit down and wait."

The two women blessed themselves with holy water, genuflected next to a pew and sat down in the back of the church. They watched as their father slowly made his way up the center aisle, occasionally glancing at his watch. When he arrived in the front, he walked up to the altar and waited, flattening out his thinning hair and fussing with his clothes.

"Dad's wearing a suit. He never wears a suit," Gina said as she leaned in closer to Cate.

"And a tie. Have you ever seen that tie before?"

"I didn't know he owned one. We better move up closer."

Just as they were about to stand up, there was a commotion coming from the side door of the church. Aunt Flo and the ladies from St. Mary's bunco club walked in.

Aunt Flo took one look at Ted and threw her hands up in the air. "Why, Ted, what are you doing here?"

Ted said, "Flo, what a coincidence! What are you doing here?"

"It's bunco day," she said in a sweet voice.

"It is?"

"Why yes, Ted, it is."

Gina said, "Can you believe this? It's like really bad theater."

Cate folded her arms across her chest. "Look at how she's dressed. Does anyone actually believe this wasn't planned?"

"Like, she wears blue chiffon to play bunco?" Gina leaned forward shaking her head in disbelief. "Could this get any weirder?"

Their dad reached for something inside his pocket.

Cate grabbed Gina's arm. "Oh, God. I think he's going to propose."

Ted took Aunt Flo's hand and turned toward the altar.

"Do I really want to see this?" Gina slid down in her seat.

Father Joe walked out from the same side door, walked up to the altar, opened his missal and said, "Dearly beloved, we are gathered here today to join this man and this woman in holy matrimony."

Gina and Cate took off for the front of the church. The ladies of St. Mary's bunco club sat down in the first two rows, while Cate and Gina walked up to the altar and stood alongside their dad and Aunt Flo. Ted took

Gina's hand in his, while Aunt Flo reached out for Cate's.

The ceremony progressed in a blur as Cate tried to adjust to what was happening. Her feelings were tumbling all over the place. The idea that Aunt Flo, the cursed spinster, was suddenly in love and getting married was preposterous. Unbelievable! How could this be? It's a joke, Cate thought. Everybody was going to turn and point to Cate and laugh.

But they didn't. The ceremony went on.

There was a noise behind her, so Cate glanced over her shoulder. She was shocked to see Rudy standing by the front doors, watching. She quickly turned back, totally flustered. "He's back there," she whispered to Aunt Flo. "What's he doing here?"

"Who?"

"Rudy."

Aunt Flo quickly turned around. "No, he's not. You're seeing things," she said. "Now don't interrupt. I'm getting married here."

"But he was there," Cate said, turning around one more time to make sure he was gone.

Her aunt tugged on her arm, forcing Cate's attention back to the ceremony. "Never mind about him."

Cate heard her father say "I do," then her aunt repeated the marriage vows. It was happening too fast, almost like a dream. She was numb. Her father and Aunt Flo looked happy. Beaming. She hadn't seen her dad that happy in years.

Father Joe said, "I now pronounce you husband and wife. You may kiss the bride."

And just like that, cursed Aunt Flo and set-in-his-ways Ted were magically transformed into *Married with Children* right before Cate's eyes.

But all Cate could think of was Rudy's mysterious appearance. What did it mean? Was there a solution? A light at the end of this train wreck of a relationship? She could only hope.

As CATE STROLLED to work on Tuesday morning, still recovering from the fact that she was now Aunt Flo's daughter, an annoying person behind her kept beeping their horn.

She refused to turn around, thinking it was some pervert trying to get her attention, although it had been a long time since some guy had whistled at her.

Was it her clothes? She looked down at herself, nothing special, a brown wool coat over black slacks. No. Too plain. Maybe it was the new pink scarf Aunt Flo had given her, identical to her own. She tossed it around her neck with flair, and continued up the sidewalk.

They kept beeping.

Her step took on a kind of spring, and she felt as though she were gliding. All right, she thought. I've still got it.

They beeped again.

So, okay, she would turn around, and give whoever it was a thrill, but just for a moment. Just to get them to stop.

She turned just as her VW, at least it looked like her VW, drove by, with Rudy Bellafini behind the wheel, his hand leaning on the horn.

He waved.

She waved back.

She watched as he passed by, and there, on the back of her now completely restored, absolutely cherry, bright yellow Beetle were the words ALMOST MAR-RIED in big white, painted-on letters.

The man is persistent, Cate thought.

He parked the offending car right in front of the Wellness Center and continued with the horn blaring until everyone either looked out or came out of their shops. People actually stopped what they were doing, or where they were going, to stand and stare at the fool in the VW Beetle.

Cate wanted to run in the other direction, but she had an appointment with a new patient in just ten minutes. She had to keep walking forward, toward Rudy's marriage-mobile.

Finally Rudy stopped the horn blast and stepped out of the car. He wore a tuxedo.

"Your carriage awaits, m'lady," he said, bowing.

Everyone on Taylor Street watched as Cate felt her cheeks heat and turn a bright shade of red.

"Why are you doing this?" she whispered.

He stood up. "I'm returning your car."

"Is that what you call it? I think you're making a scene."

"I know," he said.

"Thanks for delivering my car. Now go away." She turned around, expecting him to leave but hoping he wouldn't. She actually thought the whole thing was kind of cute, but she wanted him to work harder at the presentation.

"I can't leave," he said in a booming voice, so every-one would hear him.

She smiled at the group, turned back around to face

him and took a step closer to Rudy. He smelled musky sweet, as though he had just shaved, which, to her complete amazement, he had.

That unkempt look he had sported around ever since he'd arrived was completely gone. He looked clean. Tidy. Like he wanted to make an impression on somebody.

"Why not? Why can't you leave?"

"Because, we have to do the car thing where we drive around and beep the horn."

She motioned him over to her side. "I don't know how to tell you this, but we never said our vows."

"We didn't?"

"No, I think I ran away before reaching the altar. Much as you once did, remember?"

"Why would we do that when we're in love?"

His words caught her off guard. "Are we?"

"We are."

"Then, this is a strange way to act, don't you think?"

"Yes. So, let's go for a ride and act like lovers."

"I can't."

"Why not? It's fun." He leaned inside the car and honked the horn again. A young boy stuck his fingers in his ears.

Now was the perfect moment to look him in the eyes and tell him she didn't love him. She wanted to do it. Should do it. But couldn't. Not yet.

Rudy spotted the boy's reaction, winked at him, then pulled his hand off the horn.

"Are you purposely trying to drive me crazy?"

"I'll drive you wherever you want to go," he said, bowing again.

"I've got an appointment in ten minutes." She suddenly wished she was free for the day. Driving around with Tuxedo-clad Rudy actually sounded so much better than going into her clinic. She wondered if she could get one of her other therapists to take care of her new patient. Just until she returned to her senses.

"A Mr. Butoni?" Rudy asked.

"How did you know his name?"

He tilted his head and winked.

"So, now you're Mr. Butoni?" she asked.

"I was desperate."

"Why are you doing this?"

"Because we need a little fun in our lives."

The little boy said, "Aww, go with him."

"Thanks, sport," Rudy told the boy.

Defeated by a child, and believing she would screw up the courage to do what she had to do, she decided to go along. The sooner she got this over with, the better. "All right, but I get to beep the horn."

"Anything you want."

Cate walked over and got into the car. Rudy closed her door and climbed into the driver's side.

The group responded with an outburst of cheers and applause. Cate was momentarily embarrassed, but as soon as they pulled away from the curb, she reached over and lay on the horn, waving back at the group.

"Isn't this great?" Rudy asked as they drove around Little Italy and up toward University Village.

"I only agreed to this because of peer pressure," she chided, playing along.

"Come on, Cate. Get into it."

"Fine," she said. "If this is how you want to spend your appointment who am I to stop you? But it'll cost you a hundred and twenty dollars for my time."

"Seems fair," he said.

The interior of her Beetle was perfectly detailed. Even the old knobs had been replaced. The seats were brand-new, and the color was the exact shade as when she first bought it.

"My car looks good," she said. "Dad and the guys did a great job."

"Do you want to drive it? You can, if you want. I mean, it *is* your car. I'm just the delivery boy." He honked the horn. Two young women walking up the sidewalk looked over. Rudy waved at them out the car window.

That was all it took. "All right. I'll drive," Cate said. But it struck her that if she drove, she was sure to drive them into the lake. Or a tree. Because she knew the time wasn't right yet. She couldn't do it. Every time she tried to look him in the eyes, she faltered. Failing that, she couldn't be in the car with him. The curse would get them. They'd be goners for sure.

He pulled the car up to the curb, stopped and got out. His mistake was in leaving the car running. Cate eased herself into the driver's seat while he walked around the back of the car. She immediately slipped it into gear and pulled into traffic, leaving him standing in a tuxedo on a busy Chicago street corner in the middle of the afternoon.

She did, however, wave back at him. Rudy had been right. It *was* fun to drive around town and honk the horn.

Beep-beep.

17

Rudy watched her drive off. He waited to see if she was just fooling around. When she didn't make a U-turn, and kept right on moving, he knew she had no intention of coming back.

He didn't understand what she was doing or why.

At least he'd gotten Cate to take the drive. That was something. Wasn't it?

"I'm so sorry," a girl said, coming up behind him. She was one of the women Rudy had just waved to. One of those he would have picked up in a mogul minute in the past. But she was practically invisible to him at the moment. "That's so sad I could cry."

A second girl, this one a blonde, said, "Come on with us, honey. It's cold out here. We'll bring you over to our place for a drink." She took his hand. It felt warm and inviting. He knew all he had to do was follow along and these Chicago bombshells would do the rest. He could take a break from the stress of his insane life and have two doting women take care of him. And from the looks of the two of them, they would do a mighty fine job of it, mighty fine...but for some other dude.

"Thanks, but I'll have to take a pass on the offer," he said, and let go of her hand. "The thing is, for the first time in my entire life I know what I want, and I have to try to get her back."

"Oh, you're so sweet," the blonde said.

The old Rudy would have squeezed out a tear for effect and taken them up on their offer. Matter of fact, he would have led the way, and picked up a couple bottles of tequila at the closest liquor store, but this was the new-and-improved Rudy. The Rudy who had a new mission in his chaotic life. The Rudy who was in love with Cate Falco and wouldn't rest until she was back at his side.

The first girl said, "Say, honey, aren't you Rudy Bellafini, the gold medalist?"

He was used to the media recognizing him, or other skiers, but it was kind of odd that these two hot babes knew him.

"Yes. Yes I am."

The blonde leaned in closer and gazed into his eyes. "You're a hard guy to find, honey. We went over to your house, then made a stop at the Wellness Center. It's a good thing you made all that noise driving up the street or we'd have never spotted you inside that cute little car, and we'd be *so* sad."

Rudy suddenly had a bad feeling about this.

She took a step back and pulled out a rather large white envelope out of her purse and said, "Consider yourself served, lover boy."

The other babe ran her index finger under his chin. "Too bad. We could have had some fun."

The women walked away. Rudy stared after them for a moment, stunned. When he came to his senses, he opened the envelope and pulled out some legal papers. It seemed he was being sued by Allison Devine for breach of contract and mental stress.

He slipped the papers back inside the envelope and

stuck it under his arm, shoved his hands in his pockets and continued back down the sidewalk toward his brownstone.

Actually, he wanted to laugh at the absurdity of his life. The woman who had tried to kill him was suing him for mental stress, and the woman who had tricked him into a fake wedding and jilted him at the altar was proud of it.

He laughed out loud, right there in front of the Italian American Sports Hall of Fame as the traffic whizzed by. He leaned against the building and let it rip.

Some hero!

He was sinking fast and didn't know which way was up. Laughter seemed like his only option these days.

Eventually he pulled himself together and proceeded down the sidewalk once again, wondering what else might happen during his walk home.

It could be that he was trying to regain Cate's affection too quickly. He figured the curse thing might need more time to wear off. Maybe he should back down, give it a rest, play it cool, but with all her dating, he might not have much time.

No, he had to work fast, no matter what was going on with that magical stuff. Besides, he did well under pressure. He didn't win those gold medals because he was the type who caved. No, he rose to the occasion. Championed the cause. Stood while others fell, or some such bull.

If the truth be known, it was much easier to win three gold medals than to win Cate Falco's heart... again.

Okay, he deserved everything he got, but as long as

there was a chance he could get Cate back, nothing else mattered.

He absolutely and completely loved the woman.

He just had to prove it, fast.

LATER THAT EVENING, Cate picked up the keys to the Lexus off her dresser. She stared in the mirror. Enough of this, she thought. This has to end tonight. I need to return the rental and tell him I don't love him, then I'll walk away. It's that simple.

Ten minutes later, Cate parked the rented Lexus in front of Rudy's brownstone and pulled the key out of the ignition.

She got out, took a deep breath, and walked up the ten steps to his front door, stepping over construction debris as she went.

She knocked on the door and waited. A queasy feeling erupted in her stomach.

"Hey, Cate, what's up?" Rudy said when he opened his front door. He dried his hands on a dish towel. "I see you made it home all right."

She thought he looked particularly good while standing in his doorway wearing a black sweater and black dress pants, but how he looked was beside the point. She was a woman with a mission.

He smiled. "You could say that."

She held up the key. "I'm returning the rental."

"No rush."

"Thanks, but I don't need it anymore, now that I have my Volkswagen."

He took the key, and Cate decided that this was the moment to look him in the eye and proclaim her unlove, but he didn't give her the opportunity. He said,

"Come on in. It's cold out there." He opened the door wider and stood beside it.

"Thanks but I should—"

"Come in and celebrate with me."

"What are we celebrating?"

"Your smile."

This was exactly the thing she had to conquer. She refused to back down. It was for his own good. It was for his own good.

She stepped inside and heard something sizzling in the kitchen. The wonderful aroma of peppers and garlic fired up her senses.

Rudy shut the door and rushed toward the kitchen. "Take your coat off and stay for dinner...I think, if the house isn't about to burn down."

His brownstone looked incredible now that all the renovations were complete. The high ceilings lent themselves to new and elegant chandeliers, and he had tastefully decorated in shades of warm gold, brown, some black and white, and sage green. Plush deep-gold sofas encased the stone fireplace, with several throw pillows scattered around for comfort. A brown throw hung decoratively on the arm of one of the sofas. A fire roared in the fireplace giving off a lush glow that warmed the entire room, and Diana Krall sang "Let's Fall in Love." Cate couldn't be sure, but it almost looked as if he had been expecting her...or some other girl.

When she walked into the kitchen, a small round table was elegantly set for two, candles flickered and wineglasses sparkled.

"Dinner's almost ready," he said. "I make a mean

chicken alla Cacciatora. It's one of the few things I can cook."

"Maybe I should go. You obviously have company coming." She wondered if that company was waiting in another room. How would she feel if some gorgeous babe walked in? She didn't want to stick around to find out.

"I was hoping you'd come," he said, turning and smiling.

"You did all this on a hope?"

"Yeah, pretty corny, huh?"

"Yeah, pretty corny. Actually...I have a dinner date," she lied. It made her feel much bolder. She could do this. Had to do this.

He turned back to the stove and emptied the chicken onto a gold platter. Steam billowed. He poured a glass of red wine and handed it to her.

"This isn't from Sicily, is it?" She stared at the wine, holding it up to the light.

"It's Charlie's wine. I can't drink anything else. Once you've tasted the best—" He grinned. It was a sly little grin. "Take off your coat. Stay awhile," he said. "Oh, wait. You have a dinner date. Well, at least stay for a little while. You can taste some of this. I'm trying some new recipes for my restaurant, and you know how I've always valued your opinion in food and men."

"I'm pretty good with the food part, but the men—" She didn't finish.

He went back to the stove and tossed something green in a large skillet. She could smell the garlic. Cate loved anything cooked with garlic, and she was starving. She had skipped lunch.

"Okay, maybe a little chicken, but that's all," she said.

He went back to the stove and emptied the skillet onto another gold platter. "I have a wilted spinach salad and fresh bread. It's still warm from Scafuri bakery."

"How can I refuse?" She tried to be droll, but wasn't sure it came out that way.

"You can't." He put the salad on the table. Cate's mouth watered with anticipation.

She slipped her coat off and sat down. He sat across from her. She could hear Diana Krall singing "Devil May Care" coming from the other room. The setting was perfect for a romantic interlude. This was going to be tough, she thought.

Her mouth tingled as she took the first bite of spinach salad. He had wilted it only slightly and coated it in the warmed garlic oil. It was absolutely perfect, just the right amount of garlic.

"So, what do you think?" he asked.

Cate had to admit the truth. "It's the best wilted salad I've ever tasted. But then I'm a sucker for garlic."

"I know," he said. "I remember how you used to bake a whole head in the oven, then spread it on bread."

"You wouldn't come near it."

"My taste in food wasn't as refined as yours."

"And now?"

"I'm learning."

She smiled, reminding herself that she had a purpose for being there. "The food is great, Rudy. But I can't fill up and ruin my dinner."

"Can you at least stay to finish your wine? There are some things I'd like to talk about."

"Now isn't a good time."

"You throw a guy out of your car and leave him in the dust, the least you can do is let him say his piece for a few minutes. Come on into the living room. This won't take that long." He stood up.

"Okay, but just for a minute. I really have to get going."

She followed Rudy out to the living room, but her stomach wouldn't stop turning. Cate didn't know if it was because of his food or simply being with him, but whatever it was, she needed to get out of there.

"You look beautiful tonight, Cate," he said, walking to the couch.

She stopped in the middle of the room. "What is it you wanted to tell me?" She tried to say it as cold and matter-of-factly as she could.

He turned. "You didn't bring your wine."

"I have to drive."

He put his glass down on the end table and walked toward her.

Suddenly she had a failure of nerve. "I have to go," she told him and walked to fetch her coat.

He followed. "Stay. Please."

"I can't," she said. "I...I have that date."

She found her coat, and slipped it on.

"It's almost nine o'clock."

"I know. He works swing." She walked back out to the living room.

He followed right behind her. "Kind of makes it difficult to get to know someone with those kinds of hours."

She didn't like all his questions. "Actually, it's refreshing."

"How so?"

"We watch the sunrise together." She imagined herself with some cute guy watching an orange ball rise up over the city, and how thrilling that would be.

Or not.

"When do you sleep?"

"That's just it. I have to run home and catch a few hours now. My date isn't until two in the morning." She was getting creative with this imaginary guy.

"I thought you were going to dinner."

"We are, when he gets off work."

"What does this guy do?"

"He's a...a bartender, and you know the hours they keep."

Everything was going wrong. Wrong, wrong, wrong. She quickly walked to the front door.

"You're dating a bartender?"

"Yes. He's a fun guy, with lots of...bar stories. I can't get enough of them. We stay up all night, talking."

"Cate, please stay."

"I can't. I have to get some shut-eye for all those stories." She grabbed the doorknob.

He was standing right behind her. She could almost feel his breath on her neck.

"I sold my Malibu house. This is where I live now, where I want to stay."

"That's nice."

"That's nice? What's that?"

She turned to look at him. "I hope you got a good price for your house."

He stepped in closer. "Cate, I love you. I want to marry you."

The words came out in slow motion, as if everything stopped around her and just his mouth moved. She hated her damn curse.

She stared at his feet and said, "I don't love you," and turned and opened the door and stepped out.

He stepped out behind her and grabbed her by the arm. "Look at me and tell me you don't love me."

She stared for a moment at the cars going by. She had to do it and do it right now! She told herself to just turn around and look him square in the eye and tell him. Tell him to go away. Tell him she couldn't love him. Aunt Flo had said it was impossible, dangerous even. They were just eyes. Everybody had them. She could do this.

She turned, took a deep breath and looked right at him. "I can't love you," she said. Then she pulled away from his grasp, stepped on a loose piece of unused siding and went headlong down the steps, taking bits of insulation, old carpet, and a chunk of ice with her. The last thing she remembered was the streetlight leaping up at her.

RUDY WATCHED, helpless, as Cate slid down his front steps. Adrenaline pumped through his veins like it did whenever he was about to race down a hill in competition. He hadn't felt it surge like that in years, but this time it wasn't for something good; it was potentially for something bad. Very bad.

He immediately pulled out his cell phone, dialed 911 and gave the operator the information, as he carefully ran down the stairs.

"Cate. Cate, are you all right? Cate," he yelled as he got closer to her.

Cate lay sprawled out like a battered rag doll on the pile of rugs, nattered drapes and soft junk. He was at once glad for the contractors' lack of cleanliness and scared for Cate. Her legs were twisted around, and her arms looked as if they were stuck in the wrong direction. Her head had sunk down between two black garbage bags filled with...Rudy didn't know what they were filled with. He picked them up and moved them off her face.

Her eyes were shut. Tight.

"Cate. Talk to me, Cate," he said while bending over her. Panic overtook him as he stared at her sweet face. He didn't know what to do or what to touch or even what to say.

"Cate," he whispered, so close his face gently touched hers.

"Am I dead?" she asked, keeping her eyes closed.

A rush of relief swept over him. "I don't think so. If you were, I couldn't hear you."

"Maybe I'm talking to you from the other side," she said.

"The other side of what?"

"You know, *the other side*. Heaven, hell, or worse, limbo. I'd hate to be in limbo, all that indecision about when you're going to get out."

He smiled and slid her hair off her face. "Oh, *that* other side. No. I think you're still on this side."

Sirens screamed off in the distance. She popped open her eyes. "Please don't tell me you called Vinney," she said in a clear voice. Rudy sat back on his heals.

"Okay. I won't tell you I called Vinney." He took her hand in his, relieved that she had opened her eyes. He couldn't believe the wave of emotion that had swept over him when he saw her fly off that first stair. He guessed it was more fear than anything else. Fear that Cate might...he couldn't even think about it.

"But you did, didn't you?" she asked.

"Uh-huh. That's for you. It seemed like the right thing to do at the time."

The fire engine pulled up to the front of the brownstone. Neighbors came out of their front doors.

"And now?"

"It still seems like the right thing."

"But I'm fine."

She tried to sit up, but couldn't. Rudy didn't know if she was caught on something or if she just couldn't move. Either way, he wanted her to stay put until help arrived.

"You don't look fine," he said with a stern voice.

"What does that mean? Did my nose fall off or something?" She felt her face, and ran her hands down her body.

"Just be still. Something major might be broken." He pulled her hands together and held them tight.

"I think I would know if anything major was broken."

"You might be in shock."

"I wouldn't be so clear-headed."

"Who said you were ever clear-headed?"

"I'm lying here next to death and you're making jokes."

"I thought you were feeling fine?"

"My condition could change at any minute, and you could break an arm walking back up the stairs."

"I'm here now. We're going to be fine. I promise." Rudy took her hands in his as Vinney and his team walked over.

18

CATE TRIED TO GET comfortable in the noisy E.R. while lying in her hospital bed behind the tan curtain as she listened to young Dr. Goodheart tell her about her injuries. "You've got one heck of a sprained wrist, a broken big toe, a scraped elbow and a bruised tailbone. The bad news is sitting's going to be painful for a few weeks. We'll fix you up with a foam donut. That'll help a little, but walking might be a challenge for a few days, and you shouldn't put any pressure on that wrist for at least a month."

"No. It can't take a month. I'm a therapist. I have patients. I have an aunt with a kink."

She stretched her arm up in the air then plunked her sprained wrist down on the bed. Even though her wrist was in a soft cast, a red-hot pain raced up her arm. She couldn't even talk without hurting herself.

"There's never a good time for an accident," the doctor said.

Cate didn't know how to respond to the slogan. She simply stared at the doctor. He went on. "The good news is you're still pregnant."

She blinked several times at the word *pregnant* and tried to remain calm, thinking that this teenage doctor had her confused with someone else. Someone who was actually pregnant...who wanted to be pregnant... who loved the idea of pregnant. "We ran some routine blood tests on you, and the fall had no effect on your pregnancy. That's one tough little guy you have there." He stopped talking and looked at her.

She could feel her face blanch.

"You did know that you're pregnant, didn't you?" Dr. Goodheart asked.

She was too shocked to answer. She tried to think back to her last period, but for some reason she couldn't focus on anything but the word *pregnant*.

"It wasn't on your chart."

"What?"

"The fact that you're pregnant. Seems when the nurse asked you, you said you didn't know, so before we could take any X-rays we needed to be certain."

She blinked again, and again, and swallowed. She did a lot of swallowing, and breathing through her mouth. Big, noisy breaths through her mouth. Suddenly the saliva disappeared, and she felt like she was going to pass out. But she was already lying down. Could a person pass out while they were lying down?

"I can't breathe," she told Dr. Goodheart as she gasped for air.

He skimmed the chart. "There's no mention of a breathing problem."

"I don't care. I can't breathe." Cate clutched at the sheets as she tried to suck up some air. She felt as if she would suffocate right there in ER with the kid-doctor staring at her chart and nobody would come to her rescue because breathing difficulties weren't part of his diagnosis. Her chest suddenly tightened, and sweat formed on her forehead.

"Relax," Dr. Goodheart said. "Breathe slowly through your nose. Close your mouth and breathe through your nose. Relax." He cradled her head in his arm. She followed his instructions. "That's it. In. Out. In. Out. In. Out." She felt the air slowly filling up her lungs again. He let her head fall back on the pillow. She'd almost killed her baby. Baby! Rudy's baby!

"There. You'll be fine now. I'll give you something for the anxiety. Your family's outside waiting to take you home."

Her chest felt tight at the mere mention of her family. "Can you get me that something now?"

"I'll send in the nurse."

"DAD, I'M ALL RIGHT," Cate told her father a few hours later as she slid into her own bed in her own house. Gina helped her lie down while Aunt Flo fluffed a pillow and tucked it in behind Cate's head.

"You're not all right," her father said, shifting to the other side of her bed.

"I'm fine, a couple bruises, that's all. You two should be on your honeymoon, not here with me."

"How can I enjoy a honeymoon when my daughter's near death?" Ted and Aunt Flo were staying at the Congress Hotel in downtown Chicago. Aunt Flo didn't want to stray too far from home, at least not until she was sure there were no lingering side effects from her curse.

"Dad, when I'm near death, I'll let you know, but until then, go back to your hotel." Cate turned to her sister. "Please make them leave. You guys have been up all night. It's almost dawn. I'll be fine. Really."

Gina yawned. "If you're sure."

"Of course I'm sure."

"Okay, doll," Aunt Flo said. "We'll leave you, then,

but what are you gonna do about Rudy? He waited all night at the hospital, and he's been calling every other minute."

Cate sighed. "If he calls again, tell him I'll talk to him later."

"But, doll—"

"Maybe tomorrow. Not now."

Gina said, "Cate's tired. We're all tired. Let's get some sleep."

Her dad leaned over the bed and kissed Cate's forehead. "I knew that Rudy Bellafini was bad luck from the time he was a little kid. His eyes are too close together."

Cate smiled as her dad stood up, turned and walked out of the room.

Aunt Flo bent over the bed and kissed Cate's cheek. "Don't you worry about a thing, doll. Everything's gonna work out great. You'll see." She turned on her heel and left.

Gina reached down and gave Cate a hug. "She's right, you know. I don't know why you were at Rudy's tonight, but whatever the reason, it's all going to work—"

"I'm pregnant," Cate said.

Gina stared at her, as if she was trying to grasp what Cate had just said. "What? How did that happen?"

Cate raised an eyebrow.

"Don't answer that. When did—"

"I walked him home the night before our wedding and I don't know...one thing led to another. You know how cute he can be. Oh, I must have been out of my mind."

"Cate, it's okay. Calm down."

"How can I calm down? I'm pregnant with Rudy's baby." Cate could actually feel her heart pounding inside her chest.

"Cate, you need to relax. Let me give you a back massage. You'll feel better."

"I'll never feel better."

"It's the drugs talking. The doctor said you might not make any sense for a while," Gina sat down on the bed. "Now, I want you to totally relax, close your eyes and take a deep breath and let it out slowly."

"Everybody's always telling me to take a deep breath. I breathe just fine."

"Cate, just do it."

Cate followed her sister's orders, and for the moment she felt herself relax a bit.

Gina said, "No matter what you say, Cate, and no matter what happens, I know that deep down inside you're happy about this."

"Happy? I'm a love-cursed pregnant woman, without a committed dad for her baby. Tell me where the happiness is in that?"

"Cate, I think—"

But before Gina could answer, the doorbell rang.

RUDY STOOD OUTSIDE Cate's front door waiting for someone to let him in. He knew it was crazy, his coming over here at this time in the morning, but he couldn't help it. He didn't want to wait any longer, didn't want to be apart from her another minute.

He had walked the halls of the hospital all night, thinking about what he would say, how he would act, but he never had the opportunity.

Now all he wanted to do was see her and make sure she had everything she needed.

He pushed on the doorbell again, knowing that someone was up from all the lights on in the house. He waited some more, fidgeting on one foot and then the other, hoping against hope that the door would swing open so he could be with Cate.

"She's not to be disturbed, Rudy. I think you've done enough disturbing."

"Excuse me?" Rudy said and turned around to face Aunt Flo. She stood at the bottom of the stairs, holding on to a blanket and a rather large red cotton bag.

"You heard me," she said. "Now come on down. We gotta talk."

Rudy was almost afraid to go near her, but he followed her command despite himself.

"How's Cate?" he asked when he got to where she was standing.

"She's been better."

"I want to see her."

"Why?"

"I love her."

"Hmm. This is a problem. Everything would be so much easier if you didn't."

"That's not possible." He wasn't about to let this eccentric woman dictate what he should do.

"She's gotta get free from you. You're trouble."

"Oh, yeah, the curse."

"You don't believe in it, do you? The poor girl nearly killed herself on your steps. You better become a believer real fast." Aunt Flo shook her finger right at him.

Rudy saw that he wasn't going to placate this woman no matter what he said. "I want to see her."

"She's sleeping."

"I'll wait," he said, and sat down on a step.

Aunt Flo softened, spread out her blanket and sat down next to him. "When Cate was a little girl, my sister, Cate's mother, bless her soul, would play a game with Cate to teach her how to count. They would ask each other how much they loved each other and answer in bushelfulls. But in your case, bushelfuls aren't enough. Do you understand?"

Rudy turned to her. "Okay, let's get this out in the open. I want to know all about this damn curse. I want to understand it, because right now I don't."

"If you want to understand it, then we have to do certain things," Aunt Flo said.

"Okay, let's do them."

She abruptly stood up, opened her red bag and pulled out a red velvet hat covered with garlic and amulets.

"Put this on," she said, and handed him the hat.

Rudy took it, turned the hat around a few times, and plopped it on his head. Aunt Flo did the same with one of her own.

Then she pulled out a flask, unscrewed the cap and said, "Drink this."

Again, he did just as she said, expecting some sour, thick muck, but instead it tasted a lot like Charlie's red wine. He took several gulps.

"Listen carefully, 'cause I can only say this once."

Rudy moved in closer. An amulet hit Aunt Flo right in the face. She backed away. "Be careful with that."

"I'm sorry. I'm not used to wearing ladies' hats."

"Stop kidding around. Let's go on."

She started chanting and took his hand in hers. Rudy

waited and tried not to think about how they looked sitting in front of Cate's house watching the sunrise, wearing large red hats covered in garlic and amulets while Aunt Flo hummed "Fever."

Aunt Flo went into her rendition of the curse, and when she finished, she said, "After that, the woman is free to go and find love. She just can't find it with the same man."

"Ever? Even if the man has changed and still loves her no matter what?" Rudy was looking for some loophole in her curse. Some way to crack its code. He wasn't willing to accept this final decree. Not when it came to Cate. He loved her too much to let some curse get in the way.

"You wanted to know the curse, that's it. That's how it works."

"And there's absolutely nothing I can do to get the curse removed so we can be together?"

"You want the two of you to have more accidents?"

He tried another tactic. "Where does this love curse come from?"

"Sicily," Aunt Flo said with conviction.

"But this is Chicago." He thought for a moment about the Cubs, but left that alone.

Aunt Flo's face suddenly lit up. "You know, come to think about it, maybe it's different here."

"Yeah, we're in America, there's always a second chance in America."

"You might be right. I'm not saying you are, but you might be. Don't loose hope. There's no controlling this thing here. Anything can happen."

Rudy was liking this conversation much better.

"What about you?" he asked.

Aunt Flo raised her eyebrows. "What about me?"

"Were you ever love cursed?"

She got a pinched expression on her face. "A woman can't talk about her own curse."

He'd hit a sore spot. He would remember not to go there again, but maybe there was hope for him and Cate yet. Maybe he'd found his curse breaker. Maybe all it took was for Cate to admit to him that they were cursed. He didn't really know who to believe or what to believe about this whole thing anymore. All he knew for certain was that he loved Cate, and if she cared about him half as much as he loved her, he would be the happiest man alive.

Aunt Flo slowly pulled herself up from the step.

Rudy was just about to ask her another question when a light flashed, then several more. A paparazzo stood across the street with his camera aimed right at them. "Don't those guys ever give up? The bums," Aunt Flo quipped.

She grabbed Rudy's hat off his head and stuck it back into her red bag as she led him up the steps and in through Cate's unlocked front door.

THE HOUSE WAS QUIET when Cate awoke sometime in the late morning. Not a sound from anywhere. Even the street noise had calmed down to a whisper.

Cate systematically climbed out of bed, pulling her legs over the side first, then pushing herself up with her good wrist. Every muscle in her whole body seemed to ache and she desperately needed to use the bathroom.

After slipping on a robe and easing herself down the hallway, gingerly sliding one foot in front of the other,

Cate still couldn't understand why everything was so quiet.

Then she remembered that her father and Aunt Flo went back to the hotel, and Gina was probably still asleep.

Once she relieved her poor aching bladder, she went over to the small blue sink to wash up before heading downstairs. She so wanted a cup of hot coffee that she didn't want to spend too much time on hygienie, until she got a good look at the catastrophe staring back at her in the mirror.

"Will you get a load of this!" she said out loud.

A deep crease lined her left cheek where she had apparently spent most of the night. Her eyes were completely bloodshot and puffy, and the circles around each eye made her look exactly like a homely raccoon. Her hair stood up on one side, and the other was a knotted disaster.

And to top it all off, there, in the middle of her head, standing tall and proud, was a whole bunch of new gray hairs.

The coffee would have to wait, she needed a shower.

After wrapping her arm cast in a clean trash bag, she stepped into the shower. The water felt wonderfully soothing against Cate's aching body, and as she stood under the spray of warm water she rubbed her good hand across her belly. All at once, she realized the pure wonder of having a baby growing inside her. Rudy's baby.

And there it was. The absolute, totally genuine, completely irreversible truth.

She was, and always would be truly and utterly in love with Rudy Bellafini, the man she could never shake. The man she hated and loved all at the same time. The man who had put her under a hex, a spell, a curse that she couldn't break.

She finished her shower, put on her robe and headed downstairs to the kitchen.

"Now what?" she said out loud, as she poured water in the coffeemaker and flipped the switch on so it would brew.

She heard somebody out in the living room. "Gina, is that you? I'm making some fresh coffee."

She heard heavy footsteps. It wasn't Gina.

"It's me," Rudy said. "And I'd love a cup of coffee. That recliner looks a lot more comfortable than it actually is." He rubbed the back of his neck.

"What are you doing here?"

"You ran out on me last night when I wanted you to listen to what I had to say. If you hadn't left maybe this wouldn't have happened."

"How did you get in here?" she asked, thankful that he was somehow magically standing in her kitchen.

"I came in with Aunt Flo. We had a very nice talk."

He sat down. She went to the refrigerator and got out cream. "What did you two talk about?" She could only hope it was good.

"What else? You and me, the curse, Sicily."

She sat down across from him at the table, not knowing exactly how she was going to tell him about the baby, but sure she was going to take everything nice and slow.

He said, "You never looked me in the eye when you told me you didn't love me."

She stared down at the table, following the grain in the wood with her hand. "I said I *can't* love you."

"Well, look me in the eye and tell me and I'll get up and walk out of your life. It's the last thing in the world I want to do, but if you really don't love me, it's what I *will* do."

She looked up at him and stared right into those marvelous brown eyes of his. "I can't actually tell you that I don't love you." Cate felt a lump in her throat. Her emotions were starting to get the best of her. She told herself to calm down. One step at a time.

"So the only thing that stands between us is this damn Sicilian curse?"

"Yes. Well, not just that."

"There's more?

She had to tell him. She couldn't let this go on any further without him knowing. "Rudy, I'm pregnant. You're going to be a father and this time it's the real thing. You can call—"

"I don't need to call anybody. If you say you're pregnant, then I don't have any doubts. It's true."

She waited, gazing directly into his eyes, thinking if anything could make Rudy run, a baby certainly would. She was surprised how frightened she was about what his reaction might be. Her hands were even shaking. She slipped them down on her lap so he wouldn't notice.

"The fall didn't—"

"No. I'm fine. We're fine." She let out a little smile.

Slowly, like the rising of the morning sun, a fabulous grin spread across his face. "I'm going to be a father."

She nodded. "A cursed father." She looked at the grain in the table again, not knowing how he'd take the next part of the news. Not wanting to really see his face when she told him. "We're both cursed now, and I don't know how to break it."

"I don't care. I love you. I love you bushelfulls. And we're having a baby."

She looked up at him, her heart racing. "How did you know—"

He went and knelt down on one knee in front of her, pulled out a white ring box and handed it to Cate. She opened the box and inside was the most beautiful ruby ring Cate had ever seen. The setting was a delicate, thin band of gold, and the ruby was a large oval that sparkled with every movement.

Cate pulled the ring out of the box and slipped it on her finger. It fit perfectly. She gazed at him, trying to wipe her tears away.

"Cate Falco, will you marry me for better or cursed?"

Cate beamed as tears streamed down her cheeks.

"You mean you don't care that we're probably love cursed forever?"

"Love *is* a curse, but everybody should have such problems."

"Then yes, Rudy Bellafini, of course I'll marry you for better or cursed. How could I not?"

They stood up and Rudy took her in his arms and started shouting, "Yes. Yes. Yes."

Just then a flash of light went off, but neither one of them noticed.

Epilogue

"WILL YOU GET a load of this," Ted said, dropping the *Sun Times* down in front of Cate.

"What now?" Cate asked as she fed Rudy Junior another bite of applesauce. He was being particularly fussy and kept hitting the spoon with his hands. Cate and the rest of her family, along with Vinney and Henry were seated at a special round table in the back of the Tomato Garden restaurant on Taylor Street. The entire place was filled with laughter and decorated for Cate and Rudy's anniversary party.

"That woman," Ted announced, and sat down in his usual seat. "That one who lied about being pregnant to your husband. She's in the paper."

"Just tell me, Dad. Little Rudy doesn't want to cooperate tonight."

"Let me try to feed him," Aunt Flo said.

Cate gave up her seat next to Rudy Junior's special baby chair, and sat down next to her dad.

Ted continued with the story. "She married some big-shot producer, and anyway, they were skiing in Switzerland and she fell off the ski lift and broke a leg and an arm."

"No way."

"Come look for yourself. Says here the Swiss authorities are questioning her big-shot husband about it.

They even got an eye witness who said he saw the two of them battling in the lift right before she fell. Wait till Rudy sees this. Where is he?"

"He's helping out in the kitchen. You know how he loves to cook now."

Cate took the paper, and there spread across three columns was Allison Devine, now Allison Hammond lying in a mound of snow, with her legs pointing in the wrong direction and a mean scowl on her face.

Cate didn't know how she should react. The woman had tried to ruin Cate's life, had settled a lawsuit with Rudy for millions, and was a total menace to society.

Aunt Flo said, "Maybe it's the love curse and this time it traveled to that Allison woman."

"Do you really think that's what it is?" Cate asked, wondering if it could possibly be true.

"Maybe. You never can tell about these things. When a cursed couple make things right, the curse can't stay in a happy family. It has to go somewhere else. Now, I'm not saying it did or it didn't, I'm just saying, you never know."

Rudy walked out of the kitchen.

"Look at this," Flo said, handing him the paper as he went over and rubbed Rudy Junior affectionately on the head.

"I don't believe it," he said after he skimmed the article, shaking his head.

Then the lights dimmed in the restaurant as everyone's focus went to the stage at the front. Crying Lady Stella, better known now as Sister Stella, walked up to the microphone, dressed in a black slinky dress and really high heels, with her hair in some funky do with bright-red streaks, courtesy of Rose Marie. To everyone's shock and amazement, Stella had not only discovered her voice, she had become the hottest thing to hit the nightclub circuit since, well, since ever.

"Tonight, I'd like to dedicate this next song to my two best friends in all the world, Cate and Rudy Bellafini," she said in a sexy low voice, something that Cate still couldn't quite get used to.

Cousin Charlie's band, Hot Diggity, played backup while Sister Stella belted out "Fever."

Rudy said, "I believe this is our dance."

"Are you sure?" Cate asked.

"I think I can do this now."

Cate stood up as Rudy escorted her to the dance floor.

"When did you learn to dance?"

"Flo is a woman of many talents," Rudy said as he gently swung her into his arms and she stared into his fabulous eyes.

"Careful, we might injure ourselves," she jokingly admonished.

Just then Aunt Flo and Ted danced past, followed by Vinney and Gina, who were laughing and holding on to each other, while gazing into each other's eyes.

"It's been an injury-free year," Rudy teased. "It's done and gone. Besides, hasn't anybody ever told you that you have the magic touch?"

"Um, I believe you're the first."

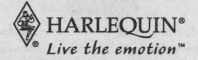

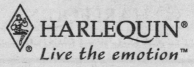

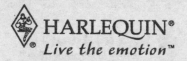

Coming in July 2004
from Silhouette Books

Sly McEwen's final assignment for top-secret government
agency Onyxx had gone awry, leaving only questions behind.
But Sly had a feeling Eva Creon had answers. Locked inside
Eva's suppressed memory was the key to finding the killer
on the loose. But her secrets may have the power to destroy
the one thing that could mean more than the truth…
their growing love for each other….

Available at your favorite retail outlet.

PSATKD

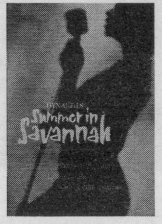

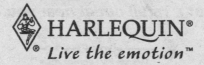

A NEW MILLENNIUM,
A NEW ERA,
A NEW KIND OF HEROINE.

She's a strong, sexy, savvy woman
who is just as comfortable wearing
a black cocktail dress as she is
brandishing blue steel.

Look for the new and exciting series from
Silhouette Books featuring modern bombshells
who save the day and ultimately *get their man!*

BOMBSHELL

*Silhouette Bombshell™
launches July 2004
at a retail outlet near you.*